Black Opium
Ecstasy of the Forbidden

Claude Farrere

Sensuously illustrated by
Alexander King

Translated by
Samuel Putnam

RONIN

Berkeley, California

roninpub.com

Black Opium
Ecstasy of the Forbidden

Claude Farrere

Sensuously illustrated by
Alexander King

Translated by
Samuel Putnam

Black Opium

by Claude Farrere
Illustrated by Alexander King
Translated by Samuel Putnam
Copyright 2016 RONIN Publishing
Copyright 1974 And/Or Press
ISBN: 9781579512163

Published and Distributed by
RONIN Publishing, Inc
PO Box 3436
Oakland Ca 94609
www.roninpub.com

Library of Congress Card No: 2016931121

Distributed to the trade by Publishers Group West

Scattered tharough the pages are illustrations of: the title-page of the original edition, 1911; the title-page of the first German edition, 1911; the front cover of the Berkely Edition, 1958; the cover of a contemporary treatise on opium smokers, 1910; the cover of a later Farrere novel dealing with opium, 1921; the title-page of a contemporary work on opium and hashish to which Farrere contributed a preface, 1913, followed by a woodcut from it.

Louis Laloy

Le Livre de la Fumée

Préface de
Claude FARRÈRE

Illustrations
de DALNY

DORBON-AINÉ

Dʳ RICHARD MILLANT

"La Drogue"

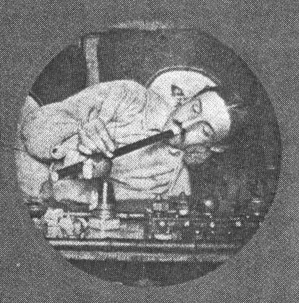

PARIS

LIBRAIRIE MARITIME & COLONIALE

RENÉ ROGER, Éditeur

CLAUDE   FARRÈRE

Fumée   d'Opium

Préface par PIERRE LOUŸS

PARIS

Société d'Éditions Littéraires et Artistiques

LIBRAIRIE PAUL OLLENDORFF

5o, CHAUSSÉE D'ANTIN, 5o

BLACK OPIUM

(Fumée d'Opium)

By

CLAUDE FARRÈRE

Authorized Translation by Samuel Putnam

WITH A PREFACE BY

PIERRE LOUŸS

Illustrated by Alexander King

LUDLOW HIP/POCKET

And/Or Press

San Francisco · 1974

Table of Contents

Claude Farrère

Opium

mit einem Vorwort

von

Hanns Heinz Ewers

München und Leipzig
bei Georg Müller

INTRODUCTION

Claude Farrere's *Fumee d'Opium* published in 1911 is a tour-de-force of 20th century drug literature. In narrative art and range the short stories bear comparison with James Joyce's *Dubliners*, published seven years earlier, but their tortured yet graceful exoticism harks back to the prose of the Late Romantics and Decadents: Nerval, Gautier, and Rimbaud. The great stylist Pierre Louys recounts in his introduction how he was seduced by the unearthly imagination and masterful prose of this unknown young writer who "never had written anything before except his own correspondence." Not an opium smoker himself, Louys nevertheless recognized "the new elements which M. Farrere brings to the literature of opium," which he had supposed was drained dry by DeQuincey and his successors.

Farrere's stories reek of opium. With hypnotic power they have a way of seizing the reader from the very first sentence, spacing out his mind, and at their conclusion leaving him with his sensibilities wasted. Just as smoking a pipe of very good opium compels the smoker to repeat the experience, a reading of each of these tales lures the reader to come back to them again and again.

The author precisely and poetically delineates the opium stone in gradations from pipe to pipe (one of his smokers empties 100 pipes in one nightlong bout!) He superbly describes different kinds of pipes, manners of smoking, layouts and dens. The glories and the excesses. The myths and the realities. The gorgeous fantasies and the sordid nightmares. He expertly describes Chinese and Indian opium, the subtle forms of opium eroticism, the character of the smokers, and the nature of their psychological bondage. Farrere knew opium the way DeQuincey, Cocteau and Burroughs knew it: from long personal experience which he began acquiring as a young naval officer travelling in the Orient, the scene also of many of his later works.

Fumee d'Opium (*Black Opium* is its English title) is a collection of seventeen tales arranged in six "periods" which correspond to six stages in both the history of the fabled drug and in the individual evolution which its users undergo. All but one of the tales in the first two periods are written in the third person; and all but one in the last four uses the first person voice. The collection begins in legend with the Emperor disdainfully dropping the pipe into the river; it ends in nightmare, with the wreck of a man who has smoked his weight in opium crying out softly for help, which cannot come in any form except another pipeful of opium.

A fundamental device in many of these tales is the sudden intrusion of the supernatural and the fantastic. Often a mysterious stranger materializes as the source of the drug. A god brings the Emperor Hoang-Ti "the first pipe and the first opium." To the opium-starved pirate Hong-Kop appears Yu-Tcheng the Exquisite to offer the magic opium of her own blood. A centuries-old "singular-appearing man, clad in the uniform like enough to those of Prussian officers," offers the cowardly Chevalier nine opium pills, casually explaining that he will appear a few years hence as the notorious Comte de Saint-Germain. Visions of the most fantastic nature routinely assail Farrere's opium-saturated smokers, who encounter a variety of phantoms with a curiosity transcending fear.

Clairvoyance is increased and time travel may be experienced after many pipes are smoked. These are among the . . .

... marvelous gift(s) which enable the smoker,
for a time, to escape from life, from his age and from
himself, and to be no longer an individual but an
unlimited particle of matter, foreign to all bodies, and
the contemporary in his own fantasy either of Cleopatra
or of the thirteenth century

—Rodolph Hafner
Two Souls

The protagonist of Foochow Road finds his squalid den
transformed into the Imperial Court of an ancient dynasty, the
two prostitutes beside him princesses. In *What Happened in the
House in the Boulevard Thiers* an amateur magician dressed in a
clown's costume and a young girl of the streets called Ether *"on
account of her passion; she needed each evening a full flask of
sulphuric ether [which] did not prevent her from smoking her
fifteen pipes afterwards"* begin acting out in Latin tongues the
immortal drama of Abelard and Heloise to the narrator who has
smoked his share of pipes and knows this vision is his alone. The
camaraderie of the smokers, their feeling of perfect communion,
is one of the graces of "the drug that spares them idle words."
The mysterious working of the poppy's syrupy black juice
which causes its users to experience an otherworldly eroticism is
expertly delineated by Farrere:

While her body is abandoning itself to indifferent
kisses, there, near me, in the smoking-room -I know that
her soul detaches itself to come and embrace my own.

—*The Sixth Sense*

Jean Cocteau was later to describe this as the feeling of "making
love across centuries." Women, claims Farrere, are made more
amorous by opium, whereas men "are stripped of their sexual
obsession," enabling them to experience a "blending of souls."

Opium is described as "a compassionate drug," virtually a "religion" to its devotees, but the total commitment of the smoker is presented in terms of sheer obsession. There is suggested the further ambiguity that whereas opium enforces illusion, it yet gives more a taste of reality than the dream called Life.

In the earlier tales set in distant times the smokers are strong-willed heroes who avoid subjugation to the drug. The contemporary *fin-de-siecle* smokers of whom the author writes in the first person are rather like certain of Beckett's characters, intellectually sophisticated and philosophical in their perceptions but quite sub-human as creatures almost incapable of acting or experiencing sensation. Liberation from the bondage of the drug which has been mankind's great blessing and great curse is a vain hope.

Farrere expresses the feeling that ultimately there is no escape from opium, once the smoker is committed to his habit. Anticipating William Burroughs' "algebra of need," the French writer offers an equation for junk: "one divided by zero equals infinity," where zero is sleep and infinity nightmare. Then again, an infinity of dope may offer salvation and immortality, but only Faust, the alchemist-magician who subdues Satan, manages to achieve that enviable state.

The present edition of *Fumee d'Opium* is a facsimile (with additional plates from the Fitz Hugh Ludlow Memorial Library) of the first English translation by Samuel J. Putnam, published in New York by Nicholas L. Brown and Samuel J. Wegman in 1929 in an edition limited to 1250 numbered copies. Alexander King's incomparable Art Deco plates embellished that edition, which was re-issued by Robert C. Fairberg in 1931. The Putnam translation was reprinted again in 1958 by Berkeley Medallion Editions of New York in paperback format without the King illustrations.

"Claude Farrere" is the pseudonym of Frederic Charles Pierre Edouard Bargone. *Fumee d'Opium* was his third book; its popularity was immense, and it went through many printings and translations. Farrere wrote a preface to L. Laloy's *Le Livre de la Fumee* (1913) and to a 1920 edition of De-Quincey's *Confessions of an English Opium Eater*. His essay, Opium et Alcool, was published in an edition of thirty copies in 1930. Among his other works are a history of the French Navy, and a book about the Spanish Civil War. He won the coveted Prix Goncourt, and was elected to the French Academy.

Michael Horowitz
Director, Fitz Hugh Ludlow Memorial Library
San Francisco, October 1974.

BERKLEY
BOOKS

G-120

35¢

THE SHOCKING ECSTASY OF THE FORBIDD[EN]

BLACK OPIUM

Claude Farrère

Foreword

Claude Farrère's *Black Opium* (originally: *Fumée d'Opium*) is a unique book. Most people place drugs into a simple narrative. "Alcohol is this" or "Cocaine is that." But this book presents opium in all its complexity. Farrère knew the drug from extensive personal experience. And as such, he was able to romanticize and vilify and variously render its many contradictory aspects.

More than most drugs, opium and all the substances derived from it have strong social narratives. Opium brings to mind Victorian laudanum drinkers – Samuel Taylor Coleridge or Edgar Allan Poe. It also conjures images of dark and smokey opium dens where "orientals" roam about, filling the pipes of adventurous westerners. Today, these images seem almost quaint – especially compared to the that of the junkie injecting the powerful opium-derived drug, heroin.

During the 19th century, opium use – at least when taken orally – was considered something of a dirty habit – much akin to the way that tobacco smoking is today. Over the course of the century, however, opium began to look worse and worse. Th. Metzger discusses this process in his book, *The Birth of Heroin and the Demonization of the Dope Fiend.* Morphine is the primary constituent of opium. It was first isolated in 1805, and then marketed to the public started in 1827. But whereas opium represented the "dark" and "dirty" east, morphine became synonymous with "pure" and "clean" western science.

This led to the superficially perplexing claim that morphine – and later heroin – was a "cure" for opium addiction. But this is not as silly a claim as it sounds. When people discussed addiction, they were referring to it as a habit. This works the same way it does today where it is perfectly acceptable to be addicted to coffee, but not methamphetamine. It was okay to be addicted to morphine, because morphine itself was thought to be okay. The fact that chemically, opium and morphine are roughly identical was not the issue.

Another side of the social narratives of opium had to do with the form of opium. In the west, eating (or drinking) opium was always seen as more acceptable than smoking it. That's because smoking brings to mind the menacing Chinese men who stood over the western smokers. Regardless of the racial stereotypes, the metaphor was certainly not lost on western leaders who did not like the idea of their people subjugating themselves to the "lesser" easterners.

In fact, the first anti-drug law in the United States was in San Francisco: in 1875 against opium dens. It was an explicitly racist law – as many later drug laws were. But the San Francisco Board of Supervisors was not concerned with opium as a drug. The law did nothing to stop the vibrant trade in opium via patent medicines. It was only concerned with the smoking of opium in dens owned and operated by Chinese people. This was just a year after heroin was invented, and 23 year before heroin was marketed by Beyer as a cough suppressant.

Forty years after this first drug law, the United States passed a broad federal law, the Harrison Narcotics Tax Act. One of the reasons for controlling opium was the "large number of women who have become involved and were living as common-law wives or cohabitating with Chinese in the Chinatowns of our various cities." There was similar discussion of "negroes" on cocaine who were supposedly raping white women in the south.

Even those free thinking Romantics from decades before this racist hysteria had mostly confined their opium use to eating and drinking. Use of this kind might have been looked down upon, but the smoking of it had more the stigma of illegal drug use today: something beyond the pale – not done by respectable people. The smokers were most often found on the margins of society – among the most desperate and adventurous. In the latter category were adventurers who traveled the world.

One such man was Claude Farrère. He was an officer in the French navy, who had traveled extensively in the Far East. And he had much experience with the opium dens in that part of the world. Lucky for us, he also had a facility as a writer. At the time, he was just an amateur—writing stories outside work. Eventually however, he won a literary contest with an opium focused short story, "The Cyclone." This led directly to the publication of *Black Opium* and a long and highly successful career as a writer.

What is distinct about these stories is that they reflect that other opium world – the dangerous one. As a drug, opium is very introspective. And it's use as a tincture and other oral forms has generally been a solitary activity. The smoking of opium is a group activity. It requires assistance and is done in a public space with other consumers. So the communal and individual aspects of the drug taking activity merge in these stories in a way that do not in the work of Coleridge.

Black Opium consists of 17 short stories. And they are both imaginative and authoritative. The scenes and experiences in the stories read like they are coming from a writer who has lived the material. But ultimately, what makes these stories so powerful is how Farrère uses opium as a metaphor for other parts of life. And he never hedges about the pleasures or the pains the drug.

In "The End of Faust," he fully embraces the ecstasy that opium can produce. He presents the Faustian legend in the most compelling context of any writer I know. In Christopher Marlowe's original play, Faustus is simply a tragic figure: he makes an ill-conceived deal with the Devil and is damned for it. In Goethe's telling, Faust escapes via a loophole. But Farrère shows us that there is one place where the Devil is powerless: the opium den. The Devil must wait until Faust tires of opium's delights. But after a thousand years of waiting, the Devil goes back down to hell. Faust will never leave the opium den.

But there are everywhere notes of caution. The first story in *Black Opium* is "The Wisdom of the Emperor." It tells a story of Hoang-Ti (usually know has the Yellow Emperor). He is a legendary character in China who was thought to have created the centralized state over four and half thousand years ago. Farrère creates a kind of creation myth out of him where the Chinese civilization itself is one of Hoang-Ti's opium dreams.

Yet it ends with Hoang-Ti hiding the opium out of fear of its power.

Similarly, the final story is, "The Nightmare." In it, the narrator discusses opium as the experience of devastation, "Death, round about me, roves and stagnates." This extends to the point where the opium nightmare gradually destroys all the world.

Ultimately, Claude Farrère's short stories act to both attract and repel the reader. And this is right. Opium has not been used for thousands of years by being an unmitigated horror. It is complex and interacts with all parts of the reader's life. But it is also a trap – a doorway to the user's annihilation. *Black Opium* allows the user to experience all of this.

Francis Moraes,PhD
author of
Heroin's Users Handbook
Little Book of Heroin
Opium

CLAUDE FARRÈRE

Les civilisés

ROMAN

ILLUSTRATIONS DE JACQUES NAM

PREFACE

ONE EVENING, in the company of a few friends, I chanced to be at the home of a certain master-writer, when I noticed, in the middle of a table, a tall pile of manuscripts. .. .

"Does that one interest you?" inquired my host. "Do not ask me whose it is, for I know nothing about the author, myself. A newspaper recently started a short-story contest; and a dozen judges, among whom I have the honor to be one, are charged with the task of awarding the prizes. And how many contestants do you think there are? Six thousand. Yes, six thou sand manuscripts to read, accompanied by as many small envelopes, each bearing the author's emblem on the first page, with his visiting-card carefully hidden away inside the envelope. . . . After a scrutiny which consumed a number of months, the best of these Six Thousand and One Nights have been put to one side, and the jury is to hold a final session for a weeding-out. Those are the ones that you see there. Sixty of them are noteworthy. One of them is in comparable—here, take it and read it.

"I shall not be committing an indiscretion?"

"No, it will be published within eight days, for it is sure to win the first prize."

* * *

Drawing an easy-chair apart from the company, so that I might be able to read without being dis turbed by the conversations going on around me, I proceeded to examine the little manuscript with all the respect that a gambler displays in the presence of a turf favorite.

Assuredly, the author was not a professional writer
That he never had written anything before except his own
correspondence, these little sheets of paper showed, clearly
enough; for they were all sheets of letter-paper, — you know that
thin light-weight paper which the English call "Colonial."

The envelope was closed with a large black-wax, seal, along
with an inscription in foreign characters, which I was unable to
read. As for the prescribed author's emblem, it was as follows:

LIFE: DREAM
OPIUM: REALITY

Opium. . . . Opium again! The first impres sion did not tend to
prejudice the reader in favor of this unknown author. The word
impressed me as having dated for a period of seventy-five—or
perhaps, I should say eighty—years, which is even worse in the
matter of literary fashions than it is where clothes are concerned.
Everything has been said that there is to say on the subject of
opium, has it not? The 1830's and the rear-guard of romanticism
have drained the subject dry for a half-century, extracting from
it all that it could have to offer in the way of the sickly and
the fantastic. The theme is one so far removed from all that
we care about. We belong to a generation which has reacted
against pipe-smoke, factitious in toxications, satanic ladies and
etheromaniac charac ters. All is light in the new literature, as it
is in con temporary art. How read Thomas De Quincey between
a picture of the latest school and a Copen hagen porcelaine? We
are intoxicated with simplic ity, with the light of day and with the
colors of light. Our very nights are brilliant, thanks to a means of
illumination until recently unknown. How, then, should opium
and its dreams ever hope to raise their black whirlwind from the
bosom of this dazzling radiance?

All this is good in theory . . . but literary theories are made to
be given the lie by fresh talents. A good writer belongs not to his

own generation, but to the following one; and if it pleases him to take up anew the exposition of an old theme, it is for the reason that he desires to renovate that theme in such a man ner that all known objections to it shall be no longer valid.

From the second page of the short story which I had begun reading, I admired the author's weird im-agination, his narrative art, the flexibility of his style, his cleverness in composition,— in short, all that goes to pave the way for and to explain the synthesis of a rounded talent.—I had been captured.—The reader will find the little masterpiece in question,—the one entitled The Cyclone—later on in this volume; and nobody will be astonished at the fact that one of its first readers was in some haste to discover the name which was signed to the last page.

I set out to find the name, but this was no easy task. The author desired to remain unknown. The en velope, which was opened after the judges' classifica tion contained a name, true enough, but this name was a false one; it likewise contained an address, but this address was quite as false as the name. A stranger to all literary ambitions, the young unknown who, wholly by chance, had sent in this short story, had just returned from an extended trip to the Far-East, and he was now resting for a few months, down in the provinces, before leaving France for other and distant lands once more. My letter reached him, one way or another, and brought him, as it transpired, the first word of praise he ever had received. The public, however, soon crowded my words into oblivion with its own more valuable appreciation. I have told this story merely to show how, far from being urged in the matter, one preface-writer has gone against all custom in seeking out, himself, the subject of his Preface.

Grouped around *Cyclone*, sixteen other short stories, written more recently, are here brought to gether in a volume. It is superfluous to indulge in any criticism; the reader will be able to distinguish, readily enough, the new elements which M. Farrere brings to the literature of opium. I never have smoked the "kindly drug," and so, am able to speak of it only as an outsider: I am, moreover, of the convic tion that Claude Farrere himself. no more than I . . . but have I the right to carry my indiscretion so far as that? There are writers for whom a single expe rience is sufficient to enable them, imaginatively, to create a new world, and who, as they toss aside the one opium-pipe that ever touched their lips, possess the skill thus to prolong indefinitely an hour of ecstasy and of dream. . . .

Among the finest stories in this book, the reader will note one bearing the title *Interlude*, in which the admixture of the extraordinary with the real is so cleverly graduated, achieved and then resolved. Among the characters, one will remember that Anna-mite princess, Tong-Doc's daughter, who appears twice in another story, and who is unforgetable. Finally, if M. Claude Farrere had wished to show us how pliant his talent is, when it comes to treating the most diverse subjects, he would not have been able to demonstrate it any better than by his description of that astonishing "naval battle" with which *The Cowardice of M. de Fierce* ends. One may expect anything of a young writer capable of painting such pic-tures as this. He is the possessor of those gifts which are commonly called native, but which, on the con trary, are so strange, those gifts which the poets are in the habit of attributing to the beneficent influence of invisible divinities, for the reason that the ability to create would seem to be a slightly more than human faculty.

PIERRE LOUYS

Prelude
Days of Wine & Zombies
The Art of Alexander King

Anyone who writes a book called *Rich Man, Poor Man, Freud and Fruit* (subtitle: "Advice to Amorous Ladies") proclaims himself at once irreverent, sarcastic, somewhat urbane and somewhat snotty. That description certainly fits Alexander King (1899-1965), whose final book bears the aforesaid title. King was a man of words, a fine example of the now largely lost art of the raconteur, and a very early beneficiary—perhaps the first—of the power of television to make a book a best-seller. King appeared frequently on *The Tonight Show* when its host was Jack Paar—the Paar era ran from 1957 to 1962—and on January 2, 1959, King used his appearance to plug his rambling and at least moderately autobiographical memoir, *Mine Enemy Grows Older.* Presto, the previously little-noticed book became a huge success, leading the stodgy mainstream publisher, Simon and Schuster, subsequently to re-release it with two covers. One was suitably grey, with only the book's title and author's name on it—just the thing to reside on a bookshelf adjacent to, perhaps, Henry Miller's *Tropic of Cancer.*

The other cover, though, bore a weird picture of a man sitting on the ground and playing a semi-melted (that is, Dali-esque) cello, an instrument whose shape is quite clearly that of a woman's naked torso, the bottom portion a pair of emphatically well-rounded buttocks. There is also a rather bewildered-looking horse, or at least its head, sandwiched into the scene. And right on this cover is an admonishment to readers, saying that if the illustration "is too strong for you, take it off. There's a conservative jacket for conservative people underneath."

The artist of the cover painting was—Alexander King. Wordsmith he surely was, TV personality he surely came to be, but it was as an illustrator that he first found success and, by no means incidentally, brought success to others. Born in *fin de siècle* Vienna as Alexander Koenig, King was in his teens when his family moved to New York City. He had some art training and a great deal of self-confidence, a combination that helped him land a series of jobs—from decorating department-store windows and painting murals for a Greek restaurant to illustrating some of the radical newspapers that flourished in the 1920s.

It was a time for thumbing one's nose at convention, if one were so inclined, and King certainly had the inclination. His illustrative art was for a time quite heavily in demand, primarily for use in unexpurgated editions of books once deemed so scandalous as to require bowdlerizing—such as the works of Flaubert, Ovid and Rabelais.

And then there is the matter of the zombies. *The Magic Island*, a now-forgotten 1929 travelogue by the now-forgotten William Buehler Seabrook (1884-1945)—notorious in his time not only as an occultist but also as an admitted cannibal—included a dozen pages focusing on shambling, dead-eyed, voodoo-created creatures known as zombies. It was this section of this book that caught the public's imagination and inspired (if that is the right word) the legions upon legions of undead horrors that have permeated popular culture ever since. One reason the material, which represented only a small part of a much longer work, caught on so strongly, was the illustrations—by Alexander King. The bizarre nature of the voodoo practices, the humans and walking dead accentuated to but not quite past the point of grotesquerie, the fluid lines of the illustrations, the smattering of backgrounds that serve to pull the reader more strongly into the foreground activities—these are the hallmarks of an illustrator of considerable talent. The fact that they fired the imagination of

readers, playwrights and the film industry almost immediately is
scarcely surprising.

In his illustrations, most certainly including those for *Black
Opium*, King was something of a poet of the weird. And in the
case of *Black Opium*, it was a weirdness with which he had some
personal familiarity. King at one point developed a severe kid-
ney infection, for which he was prescribed the painkiller morphine—which was controlled and taxed after the Harrison Act of
1914, but was still legally available from most pharmacies in pill
form. The Harrison Act specifically exempted from control any
physician prescribing cocaine or opium—of which morphine is
a derivative—"in the course of his professional practice." That
exception led, not surprisingly, to a black market consisting of
what we today call "pill mills," in which unscrupulous doctors
wrote prescriptions on demand for anyone who came to them
with enough cash.

King became addicted to morphine, he had the cash for the
scripts, and he turned into a junkie. King's addiction eventually
led to his being arrested and convicted on federal drug charges—
and sent to a narcotics rehabilitation hospital in Lexington, Ken-
tucky. King's tale could have ended then, but there was something in King's core that would not give up. He became one of
those all-too-rare rehab success stories: he stopped using addictive drugs, got back into the art world, and was able to re-estab-
lish connections with the publishing business, helped by the fact
that he had for a time been an art editor of both *Vanity Fair* and
Life magazines. It was King's re-connection with publishing that
made possible his own books in his later life, specifically through
the Simon and Schuster contract for *Mine Enemy Grows Older.*

Everything King lived through or, in some cases, imagined
living through, became fodder for his writing and TV appearanc-
es. A master of the pithy putdown—albeit without the biting wit
of Dorothy Parker—King did not hesitate to encapsulate modern
art as "a putrescent coma" and humans in general as "adenoidal
baboons." He could, and did, describe himself as having been
a "psychic tatterdemalion" during his drug rehabilitation. He
was not really an iconoclast, not really a rabble-rouser: like *Mad*

magazine in its early years, he was more interested in holding up a funhouse mirror to everyday life, including his own, than in trying to change anything for the better. Indeed, also like early *Mad*, he liked to set his sights on advertising, which he called "an overripe fungus," but of course both he and the magazine needed the continued existence of that "fungus" in order to perpetuate their own opportunities to demean it.

King's illustrations for *Black Opium* draw strongly on his skewed, judgmental, but ultimately feckless worldview. They are not without subtlety, although they do not possess the humor—except, to some extent, in a distilled and bitter form—of King's own writings. *Black Opium* is a book of degradation and depravity, but there is often, buried not so far beneath the surface of some of its stories, sensitivity to the human condition and even a surprisingly kindly commentary on human life and human foibles. King knew firsthand of the needs fed by an addictive substance and the needs created by it, and it is those needs—both the ones tamed, however temporarily, by opium, and those exacerbated by it—that *Black Opium* explores from multiple perspectives. *Black Opium* is very much a book of its time, and King's illustrations are very much of their time—the same time—as well. Yet just as *Black Opium* speaks to us, a century later, of the often-promised delights and frequently delivered horrors of addictions in any form, so King's illustrations pinpoint and enhance the intensity, the other-worldliness, the pleasures and disasters that the prose invites us vicariously to experience.

—Mark J. Estren, PhD
Author of
*A History of
Underground Comics*
Fort Myers, Florida
January 2016

FIRST PERIOD
LEGENDS

The Wisdom of the Emperor

IN THOSE days, the Yellow Emperor, Hoang-Ti, was leading his people across the desert.

There was a great multitude of them; and all day long, and every day, they formed a dark pedestrian line behind the Emperor, and slept at night upon the bare ground. They had no dromedaries or horses, and they were practically without clothing. Their skins shone white and pallid, being not yet gilded by the kindly Midland plains. The Emperor alone was yellow. Their black hair was matted, sunburnt and barbaric; and there was almost no trace of thought behind their foreheads.

It was not known from where they came.

The great icy solitudes had glimpsed them. And they were marching toward the terrible forest, filled with dragons, with tigers and with genii—the guar dian forest, crouched watchfully over the Promised Empire as a bitch crouches over her master's property. Each evening, as Hoang-Ti reared his tent—the tent of sewn beast-skins, the corners of which rose like the angles of a roof the people, their eyes fixed   upon the southern horizon and upon the tent, would descry distinctly, in the depths of the future, palaces rising, with roofs bending backward in a parallel line. . . .

Now, one evening, Hoang-Ti reared his imperial tent upon the banks of a very wide river, which since has been called the Yellow River,—Hoang-Ho. Beyond was the guardian forest, with its first rows of trees. Hoang-Ti walked down to the rapid stream, and then, for a long time, stood gazing at the forest. From the blackness of the east to the reddening west it lay, limitless and without a break. Hoang-Ti heard the weeping of its leaves, lashed by the wind, the hiss ing of its dragons, rendered apprehensive by the ap proach of men, the yelping of its tigers driven from their lairs into the freshness of the falling night. The people, drawn up in fear behind the Emperor, scented in the shadows the roving flight of genii, silently flocking. And in the face of so many perils, many of them were afraid. Hoang-Ti himself, assuredly insensible to the fear of beasts or of gods, yet trembled, it may be, before the task which was his to do, here upon the threshold of the Promised Empire which he must found.

But as the west, in its turn, grew black, and as Hoang-Ti finally stooped to enter his tent, nothing of this doubt was to be read upon his tight-shut face.

With the rising of the moon, the men who watched brought a Stranger into the presence of the Emperor. The Stranger resembled a man; but he had six arms, and his face was vermilion. Without speaking, he smiled an everlasting smile.

He sat down under the tent. Hoang-Ti, a god himself, divined that the Stranger was a god. And in the hope of a helpful message or of some mysterious alliance, he dismissed his servants and remained alone with the Guest. For a very long while, they sat be side each other, gazing upon each other, in the double ebony chair, inlaid with mother-of-pearl. The silence of the night weighed upon the earth, and the genii of the forest, with grimacing faces, had incomprehen sibly fled,—as though the Stranger had been in com mand of their hordes. And yet, Hoang-Ti was un able to make out anything upon the red face near his own; and the impenetrable Guest kept on smiling.

At first cock-crow, the Stranger lay down upon the left hand, and the observant Emperor saw him blow loudly, three times. And suddenly, in a magic manner,—a bamboo-cane shot up,— then a poppy,— then a flame. The Stranger broke off the bamboo and plucked the poppy. By some witchcraft, the bamboo-cane

was decked with jade and gold, and the node flowered into a
pipe-bowl. The poppy-heads were oozing a liquid that was like
black honey. And this was the first pipe and the first opium. The
god, with the pipe pressed to his mouth and the opium suspended
over the flame—the god smoked.

The tent vibrated with bewilderment. The prodigious odor,
which no perfume ever could duplicate, expanded in heavy
spirals, crept along the ground and rose toward the roof,—and
reached the Yellow Emperor, who docilely lay down upon the
right hand, facing the smoker, took the pipe in his turn, and
smoked.

In his drunkenness, Hoang-Ti had a vision.

Through the swaying wall of the tent, which had become
diaphanous, the forest, guardian of the Em pire, grew visible.
And, as though the centuries sud denly had hurled themselves
into headlong flight, Hoang-Ti beheld, first of all, his people
crossing the river and advancing in the direction of the forest.

Formidable advance! Against the people, the forest flings its
army of gods and monsters. The trees close their tufted ranks and
ally themselves with a solid network of creepers, creepers which
spring up even as they are cut down. The marshes lengthen
and widen, and become peopled with bloody, men-de vouring
dragons and lurking genii, who seize in a death-clutch those
who have dared to invade their domain; the latter suddenly turn
pale, their teeth clack, and they tremble, grow ravingly delirious
and soon die, in the midst of horrible visions. Other gods, light-
flying dragons, spread and hover over the peo ple, and burst in
a funereal rain, falling heavily and eternally upon the earth. And
the beasts come to the aid of the divinities. Venomous serpents
take ambush under dead leaves. Tigers bound and re bound,
and never without each of their claws having slit the throat of a
victim. The most terrifying of elephants spring up in their wake,

and leave behind them, everywhere, bloody paths, strewn with gasping bodies and crushed members.—And each step of the Emperor, and each step of the people, costs more blood than a long-drawn battle.—All the same, the Emperor and the people advance, and, little by little, irresistibly, mow down the forest.

There is no more forest.

And now, the Midland plain, naked, arid, encum-bered with steppes, with lakes and with marshes, stretches out in all directions, limitless. And the peo ple, in the center of the plain, look upon the work accomplished and the work to be accomplished.— All those who mowed down the forest are dead, and dead are their sons and their grandsons. But, pa tiently, the fourth generation is grubbing the plain.

Hoang-Ti descries, on the summit of the tallest mountain, and guarded by seven avenues of granite tigers—his tomb.

The fifth generation is tilling the plain. The steppes, one after another, become fields. The marshes become rice-fields. A new verdure, obedient to men, clothes the Empire. The tigers, hunted down, take flight amid the mountains white with snow. The captured elephants are yoked to the plow. The dragons of the air are dead, and their offspring, the clouds, no longer "pour down any but a fertile rain upon the earth. The people, their number each night increased, are becoming innumerable. And the women, gilded by the sun, in the likeness of the Yel low Founder, Hoang-Ti, are beautiful.

And now comes the day of cities. On the banks of the rivers and the lakes, at the crossings of canals and roadways, at the head of bays and roadsteads, and in the tepid shadows of mountain-girdled valleys, towns are springing up.—At first, a few timid houses, fear ful of rains, of winds and of the thunderbolt; then bolder villages, proud cities, adorned with palaces and breastplated with walls; then gigantic capitals, rear ing in the ponds of their parks their marble ya-mens and their cedar-wood pagodas. Beyond the cir cular horizon, porcelain roofs glisten, to the north and to the east,—roofs with turned-up corners, like the tents of olden times. And under the leaves of the mulberry trees, in the smiling countryside which frames the cities, docile silkworms spin the shining cloth which is the only one that men will take to clothe themselves.

The Emperor and the people have conquered.

The gods, softened and reconciled, quit their hostile solitudes and come to dwell in the pagodas, where their statues, carved out of pure gold, are being erected.

In the heart of the richest of the seventeen prov inces, the greatest of the seventeen capitals is situ ated upon the banks of a river. Hoang-Ti looks. She is not the grandam; she is not the eternal. Others shall come after her. But today is the day of her splendor; she is the empress of cities. Her gray wall encloses a red wall; the red wall a yellow wall; and within this last, a violet-hued palace. It is there that the Emperor dwells.

Hoang-Ti beholds him.—He is reclining upon a mat, under a parasol starred with gems. Servants, prostrating themselves from afar, pay him homage and burn in front of him incense-sticks, with little shells of silvered paper.

He is reclining upon a mat. He holds a pipe.. He smokes.

A sovereign felicity gleams in his eyes—the same felicity which Hoang-Ti knows is gleaming in his own eyes.—An inexpressible peace reigns in the im perial sanctuary,—the same peace which Hoang-Ti knows to be reigning now, under the tent, between the red god and himself.

And now, the eyes of Hoang-Ti see further yet.

Beyond the violet-hued palace, beyond the yellow, red and gray-colored walls, the entire city is smoking, smoking like the Emperor. The opium escapes from the pipes in large puffs, wrapping the whole populace in its sublime intoxication. Under their widened foreheads, thought dwells, magnified each day by the clairvoyant drug.

Beyond the city, beyond the province, and all the way to the snowy frontiers which bound the Midland Empire, the opium spreads over cities and country side. And behold, everywhere, there comes with it peace, tolerance, philosophy. Behold the coming of wisdom and of happiness.

The Empire is founded, the Empire prospers. The triumphant people enjoy their effortless victory. And the opium teaches them the mildness of repose, the joy of the gentle lassitude that languishes in the depths of layouts, under the light-winged flight of dreams, floating in the black smoke overhead. The philosophic opium tempers barbarian rudeness, rend ers tractable disproportioned energies, and civilizes and refines brutal impulses that are all too powerful and all too prolific.

When the sun rose, Hoang-Ti, pale and with eyes like bronze mirrors, left the tent. He held in his hands the pipe, the lamp and the opium. The ver milion-faced god had vanished with the fleeing night.

Hoang-Ti walked toward the river, and the people formed a dark pedestrian line behind the Emperor.

Hoang-Ti imagined that he was carrying in his hands the wisdom and the happiness of all the peopie. But at the same time, he beheld the forest, the forest to be mowed down. He guaged the ten-thou-sandfold-deep abyss which separated the forest from the Empire. Andhe looked upon his people, tools for an unprecedented task.

The people were hard, savage and efficient. The rustic implement was strong—irresistible. Refined, polished, filed down,—its creative energy surely would take flight, quickly be evaporated amid the black-smoke-spirals. . . .

Hoang-Ti thought all these thoughts,—and no thing of what he thought was written upon his im mobile forehead.

Then, when his feet already had entered the water of the river, he said: "Later," and opened his hands.

The pipe, the lamp and the opium fell from them. The people, without observing, stamped on.

Fai-T'si-Lung
To Pierre Louy

THE JUNK is sleeping in the center of the glaucous bay, and Hong-Kop, squatting on his mats, is read ing the *Philosopher*. It is not yet time to smoke.

Round about, the Fai-Tsi-Lung rears its innumerable islands in the form of menhirs, all alike, rising from the calm waters like a petrified army. The Tonkinese fog, heavy with diffuse sunlight and very warm rain, rests its mystery upon the Fai-Tsi-Lung: an Asiatic mystery, alarming and evil-boding.

But it is the labyrinthine Fai-Tsi-Lung and its fog which have freed Hong-Kop from the despised domination of Hoang-Ti, who came from the North; they have left him free to continue his haughty bird-of-prey existence, with perpetual down-swoopings upon the timid junks of merchants and fishermen. Hong-Kop is a pirate. Undoubtedly for the reason that the Philosopher has advised his disciples to flee debasing toil, and to be neither laborer, nor weaver, nor bronze-founder, since the mind and its wisdom become blunted from repeated contact with the same objects and the same task. It may be, however, that

Hong-Kop is a pirate for certain other and unknown reasons. For who shall fathom the serene and dis dainful soul of a literate leader of men?

He despises all things, life as well as death. He blends in his ironic indifference his own warriors, childishly proud of their gorgeous cast-off clothes, and the merchants whom he plunders and massacres, or whom he spares, according to the simple dictates of his fancy. A dark and highly respected fancy, for the pirates remember that Hong-Kop is of race almost divine, and admire him for his grave beauty and his unbounded courage. Moreover, the opium has pervaded his body and his brain, perfecting his entire being and elevating him high above men.

He reads the Philosopher, squatting upon his mats at the rear of the junk. The rice-straw sail bends to the breeze, but there is no breeze. The wan sky pours over the bay its torrid whiteness. Hong-Kop, by a sign, has just summoned the women, who, prostrate day and night before their master, spy upon his will or his pleasure. One of them opens the parasol of yellow silk above his pensive head. Two of them delicately fan his indecipherable face. The fourth, with fear, readjusts the long smooth hair, the adroit knot of which seems to be awry. And the three last, the Layout ready in their hands, gaze into his immobile eyes. For often, Hong-Kop, whose heart was always of cold stone, wishes none the less to be loved while he smokes.

Not today. Hong-Kop has risen, a slender figure in his black coral-clasped robe. For a second, he breathes the heavy air of the south. He glances at the naked, rugged rocks which keep watch over the junk like a cohort of giants. Then, satisfied, he reclines. The lamp is near at hand, dully glowing under its opium-stained glass. The jade pipe, an inheritance from his kingly ancestors, receives upon its gleaming bowl the pill which has been cooked above the flame. Deeply, Hong-Kop breathes in a divine whiff, and his eyes fill with superhuman thoughts, as he emits the spiral rings from his nostrils, and as the black smoke sinks to the water in a cloud of mist.

* * *

. . . Superhuman thoughts.

In Hong-Kop's race, there are more generations of kings than there are red flowers upon an hibiscus-bush in autumn. Centuries of noble leisure have clarified the blood in his veins, and have magnified the marrow of his brain.

And when the opium has taken possession of Hong-Kop, the present, the future and the past are, hence-forth, as one to his wide-opened eyes. The soul of bygone princes, fled from those tombs which the granite tigers have failed to guard, comes to mingle, in his soul, with the soul of princes who are later to be,—those who will one day combat the white invader, come from the west. And suspended over the black smoke which transports him from ages to ages, lighter than a phantom's wing, Hong-Kop, stretched upon his mats at the rear of the junk, alternately mingles with the pleasures of yesterday and the sorrows that are to come his lucid and haughty indifference.

* * *

In the bow of the junk, at a respectful distance from their leader, the pirates are chewing betel and playing bakouan, with shining new silver sapecks.

* * *

The jade bowl tilts above the lamp. The opium bubbles. With one long lingering breath, Hong-Kop draws the whole of the smoke down into his lungs.

And now, the last black morsel has been consumed, and the jade is clear once more. It is the third pipe.

Hong-Kop sees three thousand years backward.

The junk is no more. The archipelago is no more. The Fai-Tsi-Lung is as yet but an endless sea of sand. Beyond the horizon, Tonkin spreads its uncultivated morasses, from which spring rice fields.

The Dragon King, Hai-Lung-Wang, the Serpent of the Sea, long as thirty pythons, lies indolently floating. He sleeps while waiting for his moment, the moment to reascend in the direction of the cold waters of China, where his unlooked for appearance announces to the peoples, once in a century, the advent of a new dynasty of Emperors. For seconds at a time, his round head rears, and the scales of his rump bristle rustlingly.

The Sun Emperor, Hoang-Ti, now comes walking rapidly, casting his golden eyes over all the earth; and Lung's slumber irritates his scalding soul. With one shaft from his bow, he strikes home among the scales, in order to awake the sleeping vassal.

Lung, filled with shame, has sunk beneath the sea, down into the sea's bottom-most entrails, the igneous rocks which lie above the sands having parted that he might pass. But the hour already has struck. Down there, in the depths of the Hou-Pe, the emperor has just had his throat slit in the hunt, and a dynasty is about to die. Impetuously, Hai-Lung-Wang darts forth and bounds above the waters,—so quickly that the rocks, swept along in his course, bound with him, and fall back in a shower of stones. An illimitable archipelago now extends over the Ton-kinese sea. The Fai-Tsi-Lung is born.

* * *

More opium, more of the brown tear which evapo-rates upon the jade above the Lamp. The beneficent drug worms its way into the fibers of the Smoker. It is the sixth pipe.

Hong-Kop sees three thousand years forward.

The Fai-Tsi-Lung is there, old with green lepro sies clinging to its rain-drenched rocks.

Junks are floating among the islands. But strange ships, foul with smoke and dust, pursue and shatter them. And this is the end of those noble hours of piracy and of a wise indolence. Beyond the horizon, rice fields are about to change masters. About the cities, white with chalk and green with varnished crockery, the invaders from the Occident draw closer their besieging lines. And great peals of a new thunder herald the fall of citadels. Dead are princes clad in embroidered silk, reigning from the heart of their palaces, palaces inlaid with mother-of-pearl and filled with refreshing shade. Dead are the literate hours of philosophers, the counselors of thrones. Dead also—who knows?—Hai-Lung-Wang,—buried in the gray vase. . . .

* * *

Three more long puffs, which, this time, reach the nerves of the Smoker, rendering them enormously delicate and sensitive. It is the ninth pipe.

Hong-Kop rises from his mat and turns his eyes toward the east. The opium warns him of a danger which comes floating over the waters.

* * *

A junk.

It emerges from between the rocks. Its sails are filled with the breeze. And yet, there is a calm, and the reflection of the islands does not even tremble on the smooth water.

She draws near. The green hull glistens like a shell of jade. A silk awning shelters the poop. Large and gleaming standards adorn the sails, which appear to be of ivory.

The pirates have interrupted their bakouan and utter an exclamation. It is, surely, a wealthy junk, a junk belonging to opulent merchants or to high and lettered functionaries. Possibly, the junk of the Viceroy himself, who governs in the name of Hoang-Ti, the usurper.

Hong-Kop looks on in silence. He knows that the jade junk is nothing of the sort. He scents the fact that it is redoubtable, freighted with death. But the *Philosopher* teaches that none escapes his destiny, neither the ignorant laborer plodding in the mud of the rice field nor the leader of imperial blood, in structed by Kwong-Fou-Tsu himself, in all the rites. Hong-Kop gazes upon the approaching junk, without desire and without terror. He even, as one of his women kneels to offer him his great bull's-horn bow —he even smiles, courteously, and takes the bow.

The jade junk is very close. Under the awning sits a hieratic princess, decked in precious stones. And at her feet are many women, singing verses and accompanying themselves with stringed instruments. This creates a harmony which Hong-Kop, skilled musician and skillful poet, at once pronounces perfect. Perfect, also, the beauty of the women, who are like queens, perfect the magnificence of their robes, the splendor of the mats and cushions. Hong-Kop is ravished with admiration.

The astonished pirates exchange questions. Some go to lay hold of their arms, and pause in the act. Some bend over the oars, and remain there in suspense, with arched backs. The majority, irresolute, look at their immobile master and smile steadily.

The jade junk comes on apace. Let us go to meet it; it is destiny. Disdainfully, Hong-Kop rises and tightens his bow. The skillful arrow darts forward and rivets the princess' hand to the ivory of her throne. A faint melodious cry mingles with the clamor of the pirates, bellicosely drawn up behind their victor-chief.

But suddenly, the sea spurts as under the lash of a giant. A dense rampart of water is reared between the two junks, cutting short the combat. For a moment; then the sea subsides. And there is no longer any junk of jade. Nothing but the Fai-Tsi-Lung and its rocks, drowned in mist. Over the smooth surface of the water, great concentric wrinkles flee away in the direction of the circular horizon.

* * *

The Fai-Tsi-Lung is very great. There are, look you, many seasons when Hong-Kop traverses it upon his predatory junk, without coming to know either its furthermost rocks or the remotest of its grottoes. And today, new breaches, never before glimpsed, seem to open in his path, to close again behind him.

It is yesterday that Hong-Kop drew his bow against the junk of jade. The breeze has not risen; the at-mosphere has remained heavy and suffocating. Tired of waiting, immobile, in the center of the scorching bay, Hong-Kop has let down the sampan, and has gone to wander all alone in the island labyrinth. He has brought nothing with him but the pipe, the lamp and the day's supply of opium.

Hong-Kop, erect, one foot upon the stem, dips his oar alternately to the right and to the left. The rocks that he grazes

watch him as he sinks into the warm mist. Round about, there
are but steep bare walls, split here and there by perpendicular
grooves through which the slender sampan glides. Hong-
Kop, pirate-king of the Fai-Tsi-Lung, frequently wanders
in this fashion through his realm, and the sharp edges of the
promontories respectfully avoid clawing him as he passes. Today,
however, those same edges appear to be slipping slyly under the
fragile hull, while the peaks which overhang the fog sometimes
cast into his wake a full quarter of their heavy schist. Hong-Kop
dimly feels that the whole of the Pai-Tsi-Lung about him, rocks
and stones, is a treacherous enemy.

He goes on, nevertheless. At each stroke of the oar, his
slender torso bends forward, then falls backward, his loins curved
as in the act of love. His dull skin lightly colors with carmine.
Under the silk of his robe, the young and delicately muscled flesh
be comes apparent. Hong-Kop is very beautiful. The antiquity of
his race is written upon each of his irre-proachable members.

* * *

The rocks become more savage, the water more glaucous and
more opaque. Hong-Kop has ceased to row. Reclining on his
left side, his head upon the inflated-leather cushion, he lights the
lamp and takes the opium on the end of his needle. The sampan
con-tinues to drift gently among the rocks.—Gently? No, swiftly.
As though some one were drawing it with a strong and invisible
hand. And no sooner has the first pipe clarified the smoker's
intelligence than Hong-Kop perceives this.

But he is preoccupied with something else; there is almost
no opium in the porcelain jug, barely three pipefuls. The women
have forgotten to replenish his stock. And Hong-Kop, irritated,
deliberates as to whether or not he shall have one of them put to
death upon his return. . . . The ugliest?

At the bottom of the channel, barring his passage, a gigantic
wall now rises.

Hong-Kop pauses to regard it. Dark, steep, fore-boding. Its summit is utterly lost in the fog. No breach, no crevice.

Surely, this wall is inauspicious. Hong-Kop is aware of the fact, for the reason that he has just finished inhaling the second pipeful. But the sampan swiftly parts the water like a fin. The oar, handled by an arm of iron, does not deviate from its implacable course. In truth, the sea sinks before him, and he glides on as down a hill. All this, Hong-Kop perceives. And if he remains impassive, it is that the opium is pouring intrepidity into his soul.

Around him, the rocks grin maliciously. The reign of the pirate-king has been abolished; his kingdom is in revolt. In the presence of this treason on the part of the long-faithful Fai-Tsi-Lung, one less wise would have grown indignant, would have cursed and struggled. But a vain and derisive struggle it would have been. Hong-Kop, coldly resigned to the loss which he foresees, rises above it and contemns it. Without any sign of emotion, he meticulously scrapes the empty jug with the end of his needle and prepares the third pipe, his last.

The sampan is about to be shattered against the wall of rock. But almost on a level with the water, a tunnel opens. A low arch which disappears under the mountain; and the sampan dives into it, headlong. To the right and to the left, down the irregular colon nade formed by the stalactites, other and perpendicular tunnels are to be descried. The whole mountain must be merely a fantastic labyrinth of subterranean and submarine caverns.

The gloom is populated with inexpressible things. Of a sudden, it is night. The lamp, with its dancing flame, makes the darkness more evident. The arch way and the walls, alternately widening and contracting, give shelter in each hole, in each cranny, to weird and petrified sentinels. Then the tunnel diminishes ' and dies of strangulation. And now, the archway with its humid mosses grazes the outstretched face of Hong-Kop.

A lurid brightness has just caused the lamp to turn yellow, while the sampan, hurled forward as by a sling, emerges from the underground passage—into the open air. Here, the mountain hems in, on all sides, a gigantic circus, an extinct crater which the sea has filled. This creates a lake encompassed by cliffs. From the depths of the water, bluffs rise, ver tical and inaccessible, black and bare. Only very high up do they bend a little, their summits scaled with steep slopes to which a meager shrubbery clings. The Circus is a well from which one never would be able to escape, if the narrow subterranean outlet were to close ever so little. Any attempt to scale it would be folly: At a distance of three hundred feet above the water, large and inquisitive apes venture cautiously as far as the last shrubs overhanging the perpendicular wall; and from below, they appear to be smaller than rats.

The sampan is halted. Hong-Kop indifferently brings his needle, on which the drop of opium trembles, near the flame. Then, when the drop has been cooked to a golden hue, he fixes it with an agile pressure over the jade bowl,—and pauses, pipe in hand like a specter:—for the sea yawns before him.

The King-Dragon, Hai-Lung-Wang, long as thirty pythons, rears from the sea his terrifying head.

Often has Hong-Kop seen him in his opium dreams. He is: Indescribable.

Round about, the water is trembling madly. And all the rocks, contracted in horror, are oozing a cold perspiration.

In the stupendous silence, Hong-Kop becomes dis-tinctly aware of the panting fever of the Fai-Tsi-Lung, appalled in the presence of its creator.

The Smoker and the God are face to face.

Those enormous bloody eyes dip into the black eyes which opium metallizes to the point of absolute impassivity. The Smoker has not risen from his mat. And it is the God who goes out of his way to pro nounce judgment.

"Thou hast wounded with thine arrow my sacred daughter, Yu-Tcheng-Hoa. As payment, thou shalt die here a slow and agonizing death, deprived of rice, deprived of water, deprived of opium."

Hong-Kop disdainfully fixes his gaze upon the Lung.

"It was a long time ago," he remarks, "that Kwong-Tsu taught me I am mortal."

His pipe bent low over the lamp, he inhales his third pipeful,—the last,—speaking no more, and deigning not to behold, in front of the subterranean outlet, the rocks crumbling from the cliff, impenetrably shutting off all retreat.

The sun has set behind the mountain. The blood shot mist in the west has tarnished. Then the night has enveloped it. And the circus of death has become very dark indeed.

Hong-Kop's sampan floats sluggishly. Hong-Kop is, by no means, asleep. Still stretched upon the mat, his head in the cushion, he has placed the empty pipe at his side. He has not suffered, at first. However little opium he may have taken, the kindly drug has mastered his nerves and his blood. It has enabled him to look coldly and with contempt upon death. But as the time for the evening layout comes, a strange uneasiness creeps, for the first time, into his bosom.

He has not smoked. His being has lacked opium.

It is a vague discomfort, a muffled pain. A thirst which would choke him. The saliva in his mouth is gone. A sudden fatigue stiffens his bodily members. And sleep refuses to come.

Time, however, glides on.

Hong-Kop's woe increases. His feverish skin now shrivels. An unbearable lassitude weighs upon the whole of his flesh, and his lucid brain begins to be vexed. A vast and irregular pulse shakes his arteries. The blood in his brain becomes rarified. All his inner sap is dried up. A number of the essential functions become disordered, and cease. Death is germinating.

The lucid brain is vexed. Wise philosophy is the first to evaporate. Then, Asiatic indifference and his noble and disdainful courage. In a few hours, Hong-Kop is no longer any different from the simple laborer, plodding the mud of the rice field.

Then, finally, reason vacillates in the opium-voided brain. It is sixteen hours that Hong-Kop has not smoked. And the evil genii of the night, growing progressively bolder, descend now from the mountain and converge sneeringly toward the disarmed Smoker.

With plashing footfalls, they draw near. There are no more apes upon the deserted slopes. There are no more birds in the mist-slimy air. No more fish in the dead sea. Nothing living which might frighten these horrible genii. Nothing but the vanquished man, lying in his floating tomb.

Behold them as they come. Their funereal laugh splits their mouths, paved with red teeth. Their nails, adept at ransacking cemeteries, claw the night. White eyes, eyes without a head, bend a dreadful gaze upon the condemned man. About the sampan, a macabre ring forms and whirls, accompanied by the gnashing of scale-incrested wings.

Over his flesh, Hong-Kop feels mad and indescrib-able sensations of touch. And then, all fear gone, the hideous horde closes in. Breaths warm with putrefac-tion mingle near the human mouth. Viscous membranes lash the face and bury it beneath their folds. An obscene and terrifying melee stampedes the body, growing more brutal from second to second. Screech-owls with their cries answer each other from one side Hong-Kop is no longer any different from the simple laborer, plodding the mud of the rice field.

Then, finally, reason vacillates in the opium-voided brain. It is sixteen hours that Hong-Kop has not smoked. And the evil genii of the night, growing progressively bolder, descend now from the mountain and converge sneeringly toward the disarmed Smoker.

With plashing footfalls, they draw near. There are no more apes upon the deserted slopes. There are no more birds in the mist-slimy air. No more fish in the dead sea. Nothing living which might frighten these horrible genii. Nothing but the vanquished man, lying in his floating tomb.

Behold them as they come. Their funereal laugh splits their mouths, paved with red teeth. Their nails, adept at ransacking cemeteries, claw the night. White eyes, eyes without a head, bend a dreadful gaze upon the condemned man. About the sampan, a macabre ring forms and whirls, accompanied by the gnashing of scale-incrested wings.

Over his flesh, Hong-Kop feels mad and indescribable sensations of touch. And then, all fear gone, the hideous horde closes in. Breaths warm with putrefaction mingle near the human mouth. Viscous membranes lash the face and bury it beneath their folds. An obscene and terrifying melee stampedes the body, growing more brutal from second to second. Screech-owls with their cries answer each other from one side of the abyss to the other, while other and more formidable genii likewise call, and fall upon the quarry. .. . But in the East, a whiteness suddenly slips down from the mountain-top. And like a flock of hunted crows, behold, the evil phantoms are dissipated, anni hilated. . . .

* * *

The dawn? No, the dawn is still far under the sea.

Rescued from this abominable attack, Hong-Kop, bathed in sweat, begins to stir.

Upon the mat defiled by these impure contacts, his bruised body gleams through his tatterd robe, and his drawn face slowly regains its own serene beauty.

The whiteness in the east has now descended uoon the lake, and there is a great, a peaceful and a living calm. The mist grows more diaphanously iridescent, as the moon's beams begin to silver the waves. For it is still night.

What, then, is that white splendor? It is there, gliding about the sampan, the more brilliant under the moon's caress. Hong-Kop dimly feels that it is watching over his fever, his fever which is no longer so intense,—feels it, with odorous breath, moistening his arid mouth and parched veins.

It is like a detached ray of the first dawn; as lumin-ous as a breath of spring would be; something very young, very frank and very delicate, bent pityingly over the agony of the condemned. Hong-Kop whose heavy eyes scrutinize the night, seeks in vain for the reality behind the gentle phantom: his nerves, cut off from the clairvoyant drug, are no longer able to comprehend the world of the super-human.

And then, sleep, sleep so longed for, see how it comes,— miraculously, for a Smoker in privation should never sleep. And the eyelids droop over the poor eyes, and the tortured brain slackens and is ap peased. Dreams come, winged with gold, very dif ferent from the grimacing specters of but a while ago. Upon the sampan, very near, very near the drowsy Hong-Kop, the liberating splendor comes to rest like a butterfly. And then, punctuating the propitious silence, very slight sounds whisper, clear and cadenced: the sound of drops falling, one after an other, into the emptied opium jug.

* * *

The dawn. Then the sun, mounting with leis urely pace the empty sky. Upon the walled lake, there is now nothing but the sampan. And little by little, freed from the mysterious enchantment of the night, nature revives, hostile and ferocious, about the sleeping prisoner.

The lurid, scorching rays strike Hong-Kop rudely in the face. Hong-Kop awakes. And immediately, he beholds a prodigy:

—The opium jug is full.

How did that happen?—It is opium, right enough.

An opium thick and glossy, incidentally not very black: tinted with red gleams. One might say, with traces of blood. But the drops, as they attach themselves to the needle, are pearly as one could wish, and puff out like fused gold when brought near the flame. —It is opium, right enough.

It is marvelous opium. The velvety smoke sinks radiantly into the avid breast, expanding, upon its way, in multiple pleasures.

In a blink of the eye, all exhaustion, all anguish melt and vanish.
A new life begins. The congealed blood becomes fluid. The
parched marrow is moistened, and vibrates. To the regenerated
heart, there now flow, in a wide stream, strength, composure
and a sovereign impassivity. In the brain, clairvoyance and a
philosophic sagacity.

The Smoker quickly finds and lays hold upon his powers
once more.

The hostile rock which imprisons him no longer matters. Nor
does the slow death which he still must undergo, deprived of
water and deprived of rice. The consoling opium will be able to
soften all that, and to transform it magically into a resplendent
door, through which man, having found his freedom, goes at
length to join the gods.

Hong-Kop smokes. The sun mounts to the zenith, then
descends the other slope of its course. Hong-Kop still smokes.

And night, once more, succeeds the day. This time, there
are no evil spirits upon the mountain. The opium has driven
out every impure presence. Moreover, Hong-Kop is now armed
against the phantoms, and does not fear them, being more subtle
than they.

He knows that nothing inimical will dare to come. But he
also knows that something else will come,— the opium has told
him,—something else, the Protecting Splendor, which saved him
yesterday. And he waits, respectfully, his eyes fixed upon the east
from which she will descend.

And now, the time has come. The moon rises above the
rocks; and gliding upon the first beam, like a yet more brilliant
beam, the Splendor descends upon the lake. Hong-Kop watches,
and his clear eyes recognize her. She has the form of a woman,
infinitely delicate and beautiful I Her pure face, whiter than that
of any creature of Laos or of An-nam, is deliciously framed in
hair that is finer than wound silk. It is, assuredly, black, that hair,
like the hair of everyone else; and yet, its reflections under the

moon sparkle like gleams of gold. The neck, flexible as a stem, rises above a pair of radiant shoulders, visible under the robe of precious stones, which is less brilliant than the flesh it veils. And the right arm, extended in a gesture of peace, is bleeding from a wound that is still fresh. It is the princess of the jade junk, the daughter of the Dragon king,—Yu-Tcheng-Hoa, the Exquisite.

She comes to Hong-Kop, treading lightly the vassal water. And in the presence of his clear eyes, which gaze upon her fixedly, she hesitates for a timid moment, she, the Flower of the Sovereign Jade. It is because the smoker-pirate, disdainful captive that he is, is strangely beautiful, more beautiful, even, than a fairy dream. And it may be that it is but a simple womanly emotion which stays the divine steps of Yu-Tcheng-Hoa.

All the same, she dares; she approaches. Here she is at the sampan. She rests upon the stem a slender slipper of pearls. She comes nearer, nearer, very near,—Hong-Kop hears her holy heart, beating with great fearful beats.

She continues to extend, almost imploringly, her poor pierced arm, from which the blood is flowing in little drops. And then it is, Hong-Kop understands the miracle: this blood is opium, and it is thus that the empty jug is replenished. The merciful Flower of Jade has willed that her executioner should be watered and nourished with the sap of her own divine veins.

A very strange blessing, and the discreet opium de-clines to tell the smoker the cause. Hong-Kop endeavors to guess, and does not guess. One whole region of the occult world is locked to him, the one in which the mysterious thought of the Flower is confined. And this mystery, impenetrable even to opium, which opens all doors, is not the thing which puzzles

* * *

Hong-Kop the least. The truth is, this magic opium, this opium which comes from blood, is not the serene drug that is indiflferently prodigal of its blessings to all the faithful. It is a partial opium, preserving a memory of the arm from which it has flowed. And spontaneously, in this dim meeting of two thoughts, it steals away, in order not to arm the thought of Hong-Kop against the thought of Yu-Tcheng-Hoa.

Emboldened by the respectful immobility of the captive, emboldened, above all, by the incomprehen-sion which she divines in those unbeholding eyes, the Fairy now smiles. And this inexpressibly gracious smile imperceptibly perturbs the virgin soul of the pirate-king.

They remain facing each other, silently. He re clining upon the mats, she erect upon her feet. Their eyes meet, little by little, in a caress. The accomplice moon slackens her steps in the heavens. Ferreting rays play over the silken folds which hide the slim and sinewy body of the Smoker,—play among the emeralds which gleam upon the milky hips of the Flower of Jade.

Hong-Kop is drunk with the magic opium. His members are no longer a weight. His head fills with a radiant phantasmagoria of intermingled images and ideas, all of them sparkling ones. Truly, he is the equal of the Immortal; and yet, in the plenitude of his pleasure, one joy seems to him still desirable, . . . the joy of the incomparable virgin standing at his ieet. But she is strange and indecipherable. And all the audacity which opium gives is not sufficient to raise up Hong-Kop from his mats, so that he may take that divine hand,—which, perhaps, would yet be extended him.

The moon is bending over the western mountain. Soon, soon, the dawn will be whitening the east, and enchantments will fly away before the sun. Hong-Kop, becoming more clairvoyant with the Fairy's smile, divines that something irreparable is about to occur, that a sublime door is waiting to be opened— that in a little while there will be no longer time. But uncertainty continues to paralyze his decision,— although the desire haunts him, more and more, to place his amorous lips upon the wounded arm, con stantly bleeding with opium.

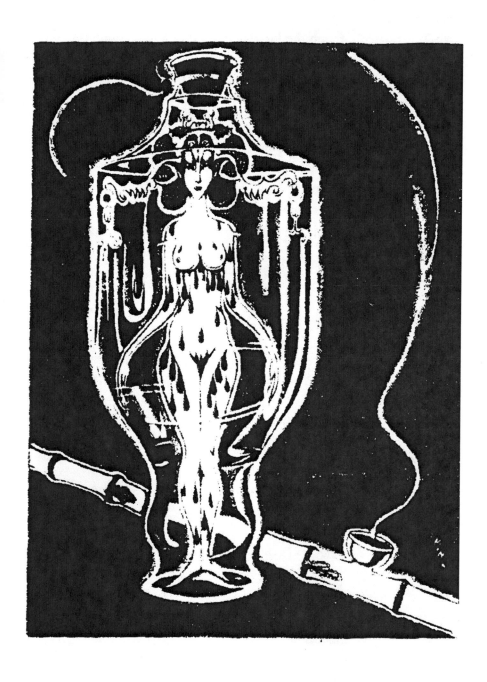

More than an hour. The moon, regretfully, has effaced herself behind a cliff. Hong-Kop finally rises and kneels before Yu-Tcheng-Hoa. Upon the latter's luminous face, an inebriated anguish rudely blots out the tender smile, the all too obvious anguish of the amorous one waiting to be loved. But the wicked Law which forbids confession to divine lips continues to obscure Hong-Kop's eyes. Hong-Kop does not see. What is more, he is perturbed and dismayed by the vanished smile, and so, stops,— timid for the reason that he also is in love, in love for the first time, hopelessly in love. Thus, time passes, without Her being able, without His daring, to provoke the mutual avowal that their hearts are one, and will be but one throughout all ages to come. They remain mute, their lips so close that a kiss would barely bring them closer. And the inexorable dawn coldly rises in the tristful heavens.

The Flower of Jade gives a long sigh, a reek of tears coating the purity of her face. But all that is over; destiny must be obeyed. Already, nascent day is disturbing the phantoms and causing them to pale. Yu-Tcheng-Hoa flees away over the sea, growing more diaphanous from second to second. Hong-Kop, lucid now, would like to cry his love after her. Desperately, he strives, with great strokes of the oar, to follow her, sending the sampan flying over the foam of the waves.

But too late, too late. Both are now at the foot of the cliff, at the very entrance to the obstructed passage-way. The rocks part in fear: for She is the Dragon's Daughter, and He is beloved of Her. Another minute, and Hong-Kop is floating free upon the Fai-Tsi-Lung, whence the Dragon had exiled him. The verdict is torn up, the sentence of death revoked. But Yu-Tcheng Hoa, the Exquisite, has been blotted out forever in the mist of the rising sun. And in the metallic eyes of the Smoker, who in all his life has never laughed nor wept, tears are born, bitter tears.

* * *

Hong-Kop, none the less, became one of the genii.

For such is the fate of those who have loved immortal. princesses. Rendered immortal themselves, their life is suspended, limitlessly, between the heaven and the earth.

The life of Hong-Kop is suspended among the rocks of the Fai-Tsi-Lung. In that inextricable labyrinth, he is searching for Yu-Tcheng-Hoa, without ever finding her. And the fishers of Halong and of Kebao are fearful of sighting him, since the sight of him is death.

* * *

I who write this, I have of a truth seen, in the Tonkinese mist,—I have seen, with my own horrified eyes — Hong-Kop — and — Hai-Lung-Wang — the Serpent-King who pursued him over the sea. But I have survived, for the reason that, on the same day, at the threshold of the Sacred Circus, I have met Yu-Tcheng-Hoa, the Merciful. And it is since then that I have come to despise all other women.

The End of Faust

"There is another sort of dream-women known as
Fairies, in Latin called Strigae, who are nourished on the
black poppy, called opium.. . ."

—Jean De Marcouviixe

In his sorcerer's cell, Dr. Faust has gone back to has studies
Many years have flown by since he signed the Pact; but in
return for his soul, Satan has sold him thirteen centuries of youth.
Dr. Faust is not, then, any longer the bald and tattered old man
who once sought, in this same cell, the philosopher's secret at
the bottom of his blackened retorts. Satan has kept his word.
Johann Faust is twenty, and his doublet shines and glistens, in a
marvelous manner, under his light-gold beard. It must be that,
since the days of Marguerite, of whom he had his fill before
casting her to Satan, many women have permitted their fingers
to stray through that rejuvenated beard, and have set their souls
on fire at the caressing flame of those eyes—revived by the devil.
And the list is not yet closed. Nevertheless, in his sorcerer's cell,
Dr. Faust has gone back to his studies.

In the fireplace, upon the red coals, retorts are smoking
unpleasantly. Some are of glass and some of sandstone. From
their cracked necks gush varicolored vapors, and it is a rainbow
from hell that diapers the black chimney. The long table is laden
with alembics, globes and forbidden parchments. Upon an easel
made of gallows-wood, a glass tablet reflects the flame of the
retorts, while close at hand, at the bottom of a jug filled with
water, phosphorus gleams with a foreboding effulgence. To

the leprous walls, fastened by great rusty nails to beams hung with spider-webs, cling skeletons which sometimes clatter in the draughts of air. The doctor, his eyes red, his manner weary, has closed his vain conjurer's tome. Behold him now as he sits watching, by the gleam of the pitch-candles, the empty arm-chair where Satan sat of old.

* * *

Outside, the night is quaking to the harsh breeze from the Brocken, gritting its teeth when the weather-vanes whirl too swiftly upon the gables of the Gothic houses. All the same, a woman, half naked under her hooded mantle, has ventured through the empty streets, and now stands knocking at the door. She is young and fair, and her eyes glow with a tender light. But the door does not open, and the cold lock resists the little, passionately obstinate fists.—Too many women have crossed that threshold; Johann Faust is tired of caresses. For him, a blonde head, resting timidly on his shoulder, is no longer anything at all; no longer anything, a modesty that is gradually overcome by pleasure. Johann Faust, who damned his soul for love and youth, is now satiated with youth and with love. . . . And the fair visitor, shedding tears of shame and despair, flees dolefully in the direction of the consoling river.

Faust, indifferent, does not even hear the plaintive footfalls as they die away. He looks only at the empty arm-chair, the burnt leather of which bears the marks of the Evil One.

There is some one in the arm-chair,—some one clad in red, whose viper's-tail beard glows, at times, like the twigs of an incandescent fagot. Some one who has sat down there without being seen or heard. Some one whose clawed hand shrivels to the pummel of a rapier, and whose skinny legs, nonchalantly crossed, end in a pair of split hoofs.

Johann Faust stares at his caller, contemptuously. One does not catch the Devil napping. Satan always sits down all too hastily upon the proffered chair.

The fire in the grate grows green and vacillating; the smoking retorts give forth black fumes; a faint odor of sulphur, barely perceptible, exudes from somewhere or other.

"Good day, Doctor," the Devil has just remarked. But there is no reply from the doctor.

"Exquisite weather," the cloven guest continues. "Upon my word, it is really quite cool in the street. By the way, I just met, a couple of steps from here, the prettiest lass in Germany, making for the river as fast as she could,—wanted to take a bath, perhaps; who knows? If I had had my way, I should have plucked that mad little soul as I went. But you may well believe me when I tell you that I did not have the time. Plenty of business, doctor, when one is in your service. I have not forgotten my claw at the bottom of our contract."

A heavy, breast-heaving sigh; no other answer.

"Melancholy? Ah! Of what are you thinking, then? You still have a few thousand years ahead of you,—but not any more than that. Sir, enjoy what is left you. Look before you leap! Here you are, still fresh and rosy, and your doublet is new. I say, did you have no better air than that, that famous evening on Marguerite's- balcony? But zounds! I surely am stupid: the pretty and despairing one whom I came near plucking just now is fresh proof of the esteem in which you continue to hold the young ladies. And who, for that matter, could doubt it, seeing that you are constituted as you are?"

Johann Faust fixed the prattler with his gaze, and merely murmured: "Words."

"In short, my master," Satan concluded, "what is it that you wish?"

"I wish," slowly enunciated the doctor, "for the opposite of what I have wished for up to now.

"Master," continued Faust, "when I signed your parchment, I was not very wise.

"In those days, I was already old,—bald, tottering and a dotard, knock-kneed and humped of spine. In my withered brain, exhausted by all the stupidities which you see here"—pointing to the rubbish on the table, retorts, crucibles and parchments—"in my arid and unhealthy brain, one single idea sprouted—one single mania, rather—a mania for living on and on, and for becoming frantically inebriated with this life which I was about to leave behind me.

"Accordingly, I sought to become young again. And there, surely was a childish madness, of which I might, profitably, have cured myself with a little rough-on-rats. I was on the point of becoming resigned, when you came. 1 regret that. You have crowned my futile desire beyond all that I had dreamed. You have made the cup from which I wanted to drink so large that I have drowned myself in it. And as for this youth, which men commonly run through in some ten years' time, and from which they rest till the day of their death,—look you —here are centuries upon centuries that I have been surfeited with it, without ever once finding rest."

"You are tired, then," said the Devil, "and it is rest that you wish. Nothing simpler. Why have you not mentioned it before? So then! my dear doctor, too many smiles have plucked at your mustache, too many balconies have let down a ladder for you by night; and, it may be, too many jealous ones have caused your path to bristle with annoying sword-blades and with daggers that were skeletons at the feast! Love-notes are gallant reading, but they are very much alike. Stoccadoes are a kingly sport, but one grows tired at last even of ushering one's enemies to the cemetery. So true is this that I find no difficulty whatsoever in understanding this latest fancy of yours. "Well, then, we are going to grow old!"

"No," said Faust.

* * *

"No? After all, there are other remedies. So, old age has no smiles for you? And indeed, it may be that you are not wrong. I admit, Doctor, that it is inconvenient, as you have just remarked, to have a hump in one's spine and legs like doublet-sleeves. I have heard, moreover, that the old, although they are always idle, frequently complain of an incurable lassitude. No old age then! But I will wager you, just the same, that from now on, pretty girls will be a rarity at your door; for I am going to make you, in the blink of an eye, either as ugly as Thersites or as poor as Job. And there, I trust, is a proposition to your liking! Ugliness or misery, which do you choose?"

"Neither," said Faust.

"By Jove," said Satan, "but you are in an accommodating mood. Are you aware, my master, that I am beginning to be at my wits' ends? You have need of rest, and yet, you must keep intact your youth, your good looks and the philosopher's stone which I, in the old days, tacked on to our contract! Any one but myself would tell you it is impossible. But that is a word which my grammarians have erased from my dictionaries. There is still one way left, the surest one, and one which, undoubtedly, you will find to your taste. Here is the Pact duly signed by the two of us. I promised thirteen centuries of youth, but that is too much, you say, to suit your appetite. Very well! Strike out the clause, and follow me without delay. —Hey?"

"No!" cried Faust, turning pale.

"No again," sneered Satan. "I have my share of trouble with you, Sir, I must say. But very well; do what you like! I shall not insist any further. I offer you nothing, it seems, that you do not refuse. Keep what you have, then, and do not bother my head any more. With this, good-by."

"Stay," said the doctor. "Our Pact is not written on parchment so firm that I shall not be able, some day, to tear it in two, and"—dropping his voice—"to repent.

"Listen. I know that I am asking a miracle; but it is miracles that the devout ask of the Other. And so, master, lacking

His aid, it is to thee that I make my request. I desire to drink without vomiting, to eat without ceasing to be hungry, to love without becoming surfeited with love,—in short, to live without boredom, disgust or fatigue. I wish to remain young, and never to grow tired of my youth. That is my prayer! And passionately, without hate or rancor, I lay it at thy feet!"

"By the Almighty!" cried the Devil, "are you mad with pride, my master? That is the ultimate mystery which you are putting in a bid for there; and there are no prayers whatsoever that will open the door to it for you. When you shall be what you wish to be, what shall I be more than you? By my Red Realm, no; you shall not have the secret. Search for it alone, or go beg it of others, if any others there be!"

Silently, from the vase filled with water, the doctor took a phosphorus pencil, and wrote with it, upon the glass tablet, a mysterious pentagram, which flamed in the shadows. And the Devil suddenly recoiled.

In the bewitched room, the two damned ones remained together, mute. Gradually, the fire-image was extinguished upon the pane of glass. And the Devil ventured to speak, very low.

"You have gone far, sir! Very well! It is of no use to lie to you. Of the two of us, it is you who are the master. Give your orders. I am not in possession of the secret of which you stand in need. Where would you go to look for it?"

Faust imperiously spread his cloak upon the floor.

"I would go," he said, "to visit those who are beyond your empire."

"Very good," said Satan, "I know the road."

Together, they took their places upon the cloak and flew away through space.

* * *

"Where," inquired Faust, "is that magician race which has thrown off your yoke?"

"Should I know?" replied Satan, peevishly. "They are men and women of mystery, scattered here and there throughout the world,—scholars armed with all the rites which are feared by me, dangerous exorcists who write with letters of fire upon the walls. I flee them, without pausing to find out anything concerning them."

"The latter," replied the doctor, "are the magi, and I know them; for it was from them that I learned the sign which compels you to obey. But there is yet another race."

"Yes," said Satan. "I know yet other weird individuals, men and women—who live in dreams, where I am denied admission. They despise the earth and laugh at me. I know no more than that about them."

"With them it may be," murmured the doctor, "I shall find the secret which you do not possess, and the Peace that I am seeking."

Under them as they flew, the earth thickened its veil of night. Cities slept in the embrace of their walls, and curfew-chains were spread in the streets, while the deserted countryside listened to the shuddering of the poplars, grazed by Satan.

Further away, the bald mountains set a boundary to the habitable land. A terrible plain, black with dried blood and white with old bones, stretched beyond. The cloak on which they traveled shivered as in a storm-wind, and Satan smiled.

Upon the horizon, a red fire surged up, darting heavenward strange twisted flames. Round about them, skinny forms were in motion. Closer up, Faust beheld strange women laughing, with great peals of laughter, about a furnace. Some were astride broomsticks of reddened furze, while others fluttered like screech-owls, being engaged merely in swinging a few brands, while still others hung lasciviously from the horns of a he-goat.

"These," Satan explained, "are Italians. The French sorceresses come to the Sabbath without broom or mount; a little magic goes a long way with them, and magic of the grossest sort.

What is more, all of them are in my hands, and I rule them as I will, through desire, through pride or through wrath, and above all, through lust."

The women continued their sport, mingling together in obscene groups. Faust perceived, with disgust, that they were but withered and tottering hags.

Flakes of fire flew here and there. One of these, touched by Satan, fell back magically into the ring, transformed into a desirable adolescent, with young and naked flesh. Instantly, two sorceresses threw themselves avidly upon him and, rivals for his favors, fell to beating each other in a blind fury. The merry Sabbath went on, with chortlings and with dances. In the midst of it all, hair and blood were scattered, drawn and torn out by red nails, as teeth bit and gnashed in a mad rage.

"All are mine," said Satan.

He gave an exclamation of pride, and the cloak bore them on in the bewitched night.

Here was a public square.

"Down there," said the Devil, "we are coming to the City of the Astrologers and the Magi, who know all things."

"Their science is hollow. I have found in it barely enough to enchain and constrain you."

"Over here, we are coming to the fairies and the vampires, who know nothing of science or of exorcism, who only know how to dream."

"There it may be," remarked Faust, "man has been able to free himself from this bad dream that we know as life."

They took the latter direction. The sabbatical plain receded from them. A peaceful moon reigned over a softened landscape, the lines of which, lines without edges, rolled themselves up into dreamy curves. The atmosphere was as transparent as on the mountain-tops, and the night appeared as a sunless and indescribably gentle day.

* * *

A small temple shone on the shore of the lake,— its columns
opaline and its pediment of moon-stones. Diaphanous hillocks
over-hanging it sunk it gently into a valley. And in this valley, a
stranger to the earth, nothing either smiled or wept.

Near the lake, the travelers paused, as Satan sullenly pointed
to the portico.

"There is the dwelling. It is neither vast nor sumptuous. Few
men have discovered this door, and fewer yet have crossed the
threshold."

"Come," said Faust.

"No! No!" vigorously protested the devil. "Go alone, if the
excursion tempts you. I have no business there, for I am aware
that a certain odor reigns there which is highly displeasing to my
delicate nostrils. Go, doctor, and I shall have, none the less, the
poetic honor of awaiting your return, here upon the shore. May I
see you soon, and may the Fairies treat you kindly."

He sat down beside the lake and brushed the water with his
forked foot. The water at once began to boil.

Faust climbed the steps of the temple. Above the door, a
carved motto caught his eye: Neither God nor Devil. For a
second, he hesitated, with upraised hand.

Then he pushed in the door, which offered no resistance.

* * *

In the temple, there was no altar nor statue nor anything of
mystery. The fairies are not decked in precious stones and carry
no wands or distaffs.

These are simple women, or at least, they appear to be. Their
supple bodies are scattered over the couches in an abandonment
of repose. Their serene mouths smile toward the invisible, and
their clear eyes follow, without tiring, the energetic flight of
dreams, hovering under the sacred vault.

Between the flagstones of flaxen-colored shell, singular
plants take root; and it is a bizarre flora which blooms throughout

the temple, like wheat in a field. Tall stalks rise, weighted down with long, wide leaves; the flowers sway, deep as cups, and black.

Sometimes, with a slow gesture, one of the Vampires stretches forth her bare arm and plucks the nearest flower. She breathes it in for long, then lifts it to her lips and sucks the black juice which pearls upon the edge of each petal.

Faust has exclaimed: I am here. But the Fairies have not heard him, and have not gazed in his direction. They are dreaming, and eating the flowers of the black poppy.

Faust is silent. He, in his turn, looks up toward the vault, and breathes in, surprisedly, the perfume which spreads from the corollas. An imperceptible drunkenness worms its way through his nostrils and glides to his brain,—from the start.

The vault, assuredly, is empty.—Those are but vapors floating along the frieze and spreading out in intermingled scrolls.—But those scrolls coil in strange fashions.—They are iridescent with a multitude of colors. They clothe themselves with singular forms, indefinite, by turns, and precise.—And these phantoms, never before seen, begin to move and to live.— Dream-scenes are written and effaced within the period of a sigh, and are reborn, and metamorphosed. —Scenes light and fugitive,—then clearer. A mist-dream,—then limpid,—then real,—as real as the reality of life,—more real. . . .

. . . Faust, dazzled, looks on.

Near his lips, a large flower has bloomed, temptingly. A potent odor rises from the opened corolla. Faust, with the slow gesture of the Vampires, pulls off the first petal,—and, little by little, brings it nearer his opened mouth. . . .

* * *

It is a thousand years ago that Doctor Faust entered the opaline temple. On the shore of the parched lake, the Devil is waiting still.

Doctor Faust has not come out.

The pact is long overdue. From the height of the firmament, the ironic moon draws long horns behind Satan's shadow.

The Devil, in a rage, occasionally approaches the portico. But at once, he recoils. At this threshold, his power expires;—nothing within belongs to him.

And the Devil goes back to his seat upon the bluff of the lake. His goat-feet have hollowed red holes in the soil, and glowing coals shoot forth about him.

He will very soon fall back, all alone, into Hell.

SECOND PERIOD
ANNALS

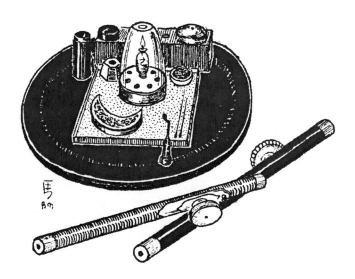

The Cowardice of Monsieur de Fierce

That the late comte de Fierce had been a cuckold, no one doubted, in the city any more than at the court. But the authentic list of those who had assisted him in becoming one, few would have been able to compile, for the countess had shown herself to be, always, as secretive as she was fickle. And now, moreover, grown old and prudish, she had retreated to the privacy of her estate in Dauphiny, and there was giving herself to God, since men would have no more to do with her. The cuckoldoms of yesteryear were, accordingly, veiled in distance. But the gossips, who are never lacking to the scene, by no means had laid down their arms as yet. And since the chief glory of a beauty lies in the quality of her intrigues, it was a common subject of remark that, frequently, the poor lady's favorites had not been such as to give her any great cause for pride, seeing that, even though some of them might have been great lords, many others had been no more than little flunkies.

The truth is, this was a wholly unjustified inference, and one due, it may be, to the vindictive spite of a few old beaux, formerly repulsed by Madame de Fierce. Nevertheless, the calumny assumed the appearance of truth, when one recalled the strange and scandalous life which the chevalier, the countess' younger son, was leading at court;—scandalous to such a degree that it seemed to point to a true lackey, rather than to the scion of a race of noble gentlemen, who were well known among the best families of the realm. .. .

It goes without saying that there is no allusion here to the count's elder son, who was later Marshal of France, after having wed Mademoiselle de Parthenay, bastard of the King;—but merely to his younger brother, the Chevalier Jean, whose career, as will be seen, was a brief one.

Well, then,—and all this took place in the spring of the year 1747,—the Chevalier de Fierce, having been, provided by his brother with a suitable portion, was presented to the King and took due rank at court. His Majesty, for that matter, already had heard of him, having, out of his great kindness, made the youth a present, upon the death of the late count, of a vacant regiment. And so, it came about that M. de Fierce, who had had no military experience, found himself, none the less, from his fifteenth year, colonel of three hundred amaranthine dragoons. And the King, who had a good memory, reminded M. de Fierce of this, upon the latter's presentation at court, —trusting, he said, that the Chevalier would take care, upon the field of battle, not merely to sustain the honor of his house, but to add to that honor.

This seemed to predict for M. de Fierce a brilliant future at the trade of arms, whither the royal favor appeared thus to be propelling him; and yet, the chevalier was in no haste to rejoin his regiment, which at that moment was engaged in fighting in Germany. And every one was greatly surprised, when it became known that, in spite of all appearance of likelihood, M. de Fierce most absurdly had asked for a pacific barracks post, which would not necessitate his leaving the court. Still, a younger brother could not hope to cut a very great figure. A song began to make the rounds, lauding the prudence of a certain new Ulysses whose name was Jean. The King, for all that, did not concern himself in the matter, but granted his Colonel's request,—disdainfully, some said.

After all, there was nothing in this that was exactly dishonorable. Many schemers at court were willing to accept the most ordinary of futures, providing that future kept them near the

King, the source of all great fortune. But in the present instance,
the gossiping tongues soon discovered that the Chevalier Jean
was not a schemer, and that ambition had no dwelling-place
in his soul. His desires, in truth, were limited to his creature
comforts, without his being able to descry, seemingly, any other
glory than those of bed and board. Not that he was stupid. But
his mind, sufficiently alert and subtle, took an especial pleasure
in ruses, knaveries and artifices, as well as in gluttony and
playing the jolly dog, all of which is characteristic of those of
lowest extraction; bold and perilous cabals appeared, really,
to frighten him. All these being instincts which evidenced
an exceedingly vulgar worth. The poets love to compare the
members of the nobility to those courageous beasts which are to
be seen on coats-of-arms and other heraldic devices,—such as
lions, unicorns and leopards. But to tell the truth, if it had been
a case of finding some little animal whose equal in valor M. de
Fierce was, one would have had to look among the less heraldic
creatures, such as pheasants, hares or frogs.

To put it all in a word, M. de Fierce was a poltroon; and
the court at once knew, precisely, what opinion to adopt on this
score.

The first incident to reveal this poltroonery came to light
barely three months after M. de Fierce had been presented at
court. At this period, the chevalier, who was possessed of neither
a bad figure nor an ugly face, had been singled out by Madame
de Cossac, who still was "coming" forty, and who found her
chief pleasure in playing with the fire of youth, in the persons
of the youngest of the young gentlemen at court. The marquis,
who was built for the part, shut his eyes so accurately that he,
commonly, was the only one who perceived nothing of what
went on. But unfortunate circumstance would have it that, this
once, he should see everything, and wholly in spite of himself.
Greatly put out at a discovery which obliged him to play the
abused, the old lord thought, at first, of petitioning the King for

an arbitrary warrant of imprisonment for the unfaithful lady,
and another one for her seducer. But upon consideration, the
great reputation of the late Comte de Fierce, a portion of which
was reflected upon the younger son, dismayed the marquis. To
such an extent that, overlooking the some thirty years difference
between his own age and that of the youngster, M. de Cossac
challenged the latter. The court, watching the affair closely,
marveled no end at the great kindness of the marquis and the
unusual honor he was conferring upon his adversary, a mere
younger son. M. de Fierce's reputation at once shot up, and that
very evening, a number of ladies, and by no means of the least in
rank, addressed to him gracious little notes, conveying their best
wishes for his victory, at the same time offering, more or less
indiscreetly, to supplant in his heart the charms of the somewhat
superannuated marquise. A number of gentlemen, on the other
hand, desirous of being parties to a duel which promised to be
the last word in gallantry, besought the chevalier to accept them
as his seconds.

But the chevalier did not fight. During the night preceding the
encounter, he fell the full length of some stair or other and broke
his leg. M. de Cossac, in accordance with the rules of courtesy,
made haste to dispatch his own physicians. The latter found the
injured man in bed, his knee wrapped up in bandages, and with
two Swiss surgeons at his side. But when they wished to examine
the wound, M. de Fierce so vigorously opposed the proceeding
that certain doubts began to take shape in their minds. The
half-serious, half-jocular attitude of the two Helvetians was all
that was needed to confirm their suspicions. They, accordingly,
returned to the marquis, announcing to any who cared to listen
that the patient they had visited was doing wonderfully well, with
the exception of one very grave malady which had hold of him,
but which they had not undertaken to cure, namely,—fear.

M. de Cossac, justly indignant, made a great to-do about the
matter. But this was unfortunate for him, since the Comte de

Fierce, concerned for the family honor, offered himself as his
brother's surety and, in turn, challenged the marquis. They went
out upon the green, and M. de Cossac was slain. The scandal at
once died down, though it might, very well, have started up all
over again, seeing that, by a miracle, the chevalier found himself
cured and leg-whole two days after his adversary's death.

But if his brother's duel with the count had whitewashed the
chevalier's reputation, this was but for a time.

Indeed, some weeks later, official duties brought M. de Fierce
to Paris. It was a matter having to do with certain documents,
which the King had addressed to the governor of the Bastille.
Nothing, otherwise, of any great importance; so that the chevalier
set out in a carriage, with no escort, being armed only with
pistols, which gave certain gentlemen of the guard the idea of
indulging in a merry little hoax.

The chevalier, who had no suspicion of what was up, had
delivered his message and was returning in great haste, bringing
with him a sealed packet for His Majesty. Well, the night being
dark, the rainfall heavy and the road a deserted one, M. de
Fierce thought he would die of fright, as he heard, of a sudden, a
fusillade of pistols, and felt his carriage, at the same time, being
brought to a stop with a frightful jolt. It was even worse, as, by
the gleam of lanterns, he perceived four horsemen, duly masked,
threatening his flunkies with their weapons. There was, in truth,
no need of this, since the rabble gave themselves up at once,
without resistance. And at the command of one of the aggressors,
M. de Fierce, more dead than alive, was forced to climb down
and docilely follow his conquerors into the woods.

There, he was enjoined to throw away his pistols and his
sword, which he very readily did. He was then ordered to give
up his letters, which he likewise did without resistance. Lastly,
he was commanded to let down his clothes, which frightened
him greatly. Then, the masked men held a conference, in a low
tone of voice, and appeared to reach an agreement, signifying to

him that they were about to slay him. At this, the scene became a pitiful one. M. de Fierce threw himself to his knees and begged, as humbly as any one could, to be spared, swearing a thousand oaths that he never would breathe a word of the incident, and suggesting the most extravagant ransoms. Since no one seemed to be affected by his supplications, M. de Fierce began imploring his four executioners, one after another, crawling to their feet and kissing their hands like holy rehcs. It was not till then that the mysterious horsemen softened to the extent of showing him mercy, when, all of a sudden, they galloped away, leaving their victim grimy with mud, drenched with rain and trickling with tears,— in short, in a most pitiable plight, indeed.

Shaking all over with fear, M. de Fierce ran through the woods all the way to Versailles, not feeling safe until he once had lifted his own latch. But he was terribly confused to find what awaited him: upon his table was the King's packet, intact, and beside it an ironic cartel from the four officers, a quartette of practical jokers who had been having sport with him.

This affair was not greatly noised about, since none of those who had played a part in it cared greatly about having it reach the ears of the King. However, M. de Fierce lost the little consideration which he previously had enjoyed. And the first unpleasant rumor that followed necessarily ratified his disgrace.

This time, the scandal was such that His Majesty could not ignore it. One evening, at the King's own gaming-board, the chevalier, whose servile soul persisted in protruding through his gallant-fellow's frock, felt called upon to remark that his opponent, who happened to be the Comte de Gurcy, was playing the game unfairly. With the most incredible bad taste, M. de Fierce called upon all the spectators to be his witnesses, which earned him a handsome slap from the count's hand. None took the trouble to interpose, when, to the utter astonishment of all, the chevalier, accepting without flinching the unbearable insult which had been offered him, begged M. de Gurcy, in Christian

fashion, to accept his excuses, assuring the latter that he had
had no intention of giving offense, and that he cherished no
grudge as a result of the count's justifiable sprightliness. There
was an impressive silence; and the King, who had just been
informed of what had happened, leaped up at once, as though the
shameful conduct of one of his gentlemen had, in some manner,
bespattered his own ermine cloak. M. de Fierce, as the others
hastily withdrew, found himself left alone, like a sort of plague-
victim.

The King now lost no time in evincing his displeasure. At
the royal levee the next morning, as His Majesty was leaving his
apartments, a group of courtiers came to offer their greetings, and
the Chevalier de Fierce had the audacity to take his place among
them. But the King, singling him out at once, strode directly up
to him and, in an ironical speech, expressed his astonishment that
so brave a gentleman, and one so ticklish in all points touching
his honor, could linger like that in idleness, whilst the whole of
Europe was engaged in a bloody warfare.

"Are you not, moreover," added His Majesty, "the colonel
of one of our regiments? By that, we do not mean to imply that
you should rejoin it at once, for it is fighting in the heart of
Franconia, and such courage as yours would, no doubt, find the
least delay repugnant. But we have not the slightest doubt that a
soldier such as you is as fitted for battles at sea as he is for those
on terra firma. And that is why, our Rochef ort fleet being ready
to set sail, you are to join it at once. The marquis de l'Estanduere,
who is in command, will provide you with the opportunity of
distinguishing yourself, by assigning you some post that is
worthy,—not, to be sure, of your courage, but at least of your
birth, and of the rank which you have held, up to now."

"Sire," stammered the chevalier, turning very pale, "Your
Majesty overwhelms me. . . ."

But already, the King, without, deigning even to touch his
hat-brim, had stalked away in disdain.

There was nothing to do but obey. M. de Fierce, highly
distressed and in a tremor of fear, went to say goodby to
the nymphs in the park, upon whom he bestowed a special
friendship. The appearance, at once rustic and royal, of these
groves, bearing witness to a vanished peace of mind, did not fail
to move him to the point of tears. Confident of his solitude, he
fell to weeping outright, leaning against the pedestal of a marble
beauty, when someone whose footsteps he had not heard stood,
suddenly, coughing before him.

Taken by surprise and thrown into confusion, the chevalier
drew himself up and strove to compose his features. He
thereupon perceived, at a distance of less than six paces, a
singular-appearing man, clad in a uniform like enough to those of
Prussian officers. The stranger stood gazing at him, fixedly, with
immobile eyes. M. de Fierce never had seen the fellow, anywhere
before.

"Whom, then," he inquired, still with some surprise, "have I
the honor of addressing?"

The stranger smiled and gently shrugged his shoulders.

"Some one who wishes you well, Monsieur le Chevalier de
Fierce, and who would like to prove it."

"How do you know my name?"

"I know all names."

"In that case, I fancy, you will not refuse to tell me yours."

"I have none. However, if it pleases you to give me one, call
me the Marquis de Montferrat."

M. de Fierce gazed with curiosity at this stranger, who had
thus made himself a present of a mar-quisate. Nothing highly
extraordinary was to be discovered about him. And yet, his eyes,
weirdly cold and clear, did not resemble any other eyes, while
the mask which was his face exhibited an impassivity which no
likely span of years could have written there.

"Sir," said the chevalier at last, "I am listening."

The Marquis de Montferrat sat down upon a bench, threw his right leg across his left, rested his chin in his hand and began:

"Sir, I am aware, to the slightest detail, of all the events which have gone to make up your life; and if I thought it at all useful, I even could reveal to you a number of incidents which have happened without your knowing of them,—that of your birth, to begin with. I shall do nothing of the sort, however, for reasons having to do with wisdom and discretion. I could, with almost equal ease, enlighten you with regard to the future that awaits you. But it is infinitely preferable that you continue in your ignorance. That is why, although I happen to be a sorcerer,—and, I might add, a sorcerer of some merit, —I am not here, by any means, to talk to you about the future, any more than I am to talk about the present or the past. It is best to forget all those things, or to remain in ignorance of them. No, my visit has a less frivolous motive: it is given me to render you today a signal service,—providing only you give your consent."

The chevalier listened with gaping mouth, even more alarmed than surprised.

"Very well, sir, let us come to the point," continued the sorcerer, after a pause. "I have told you that nothing in your history is dark to me. That being so, I am acquainted, better than any man in France, better even than King Louis XV., who drove you from his Court this morning, with the regrettable incidents which have brought to light that particular one of your virtues which it would have been the greatest prudence modestly to conceal,—I mean, cowardice, baseness, contemptibility, of which you are a shining example."

"Sir!" protested the chevalier, struck to the quick.

"Do not take offense. Endeavor, rather, to look upon me as upon a fraction of yourself, or if it pleases you better, as the guardian angel who, as you know, is attached to your person. Like him, I am able to fathom the least of your thoughts. Have no shame, therefore, in hearing me reveal them without any word-mincing, as I discourse in a loud voice of those intimate secrets which you would prefer to keep from yourself. The forms of politeness and the lying manners of good society have no place here between us.

"Well, then, Monsieur le Chevalier, you are a poltroon of a rare sort, one better fitted to wear laced livery than a sword. On the other hand, here you are, condemned to leave for war, where bravery is still quite fashionable. What are you going to do there? That is what concerns me. Such deeds, perhaps, as will cause your coat-of-arms to be unfavorably stained and tarnished,—that coat-of-arms which consists of a golden chevron on an azure field, accompanied by three nefs of the same color, two and one, riding upon a sea of silver. That would displease me very much. I have resolved, accordingly, to summon my art to the rescue; and I have come to offer you an infallible charm, one wonderfully adapted to routing all your fears, whatever day and hour you please."

"Sir," said the chevalier, "you are indulging in a pleasant hoax."

The marquis-sorcerer grew warm at this.

"No, sir, I am not indulging in any hoax whatsoever; and what is more, it seems to me that you are audacious and ill-advised to pretend to have a strong and a sceptical mind on the subject of these authentic and altogether to-be-dreaded secrets. Take care, rather, to preserve your silence and your fear; for these secrets, which today condescend to aid you, might very well, as you know, become irritated by your mockery and turn against you; in which case, I would not give a Spanish maravedi for your hide."

The chevalier did not breathe.

"In a few words," concluded the speaker, "what I have to say to you is: this dish contains certain globules or pills, composed of a tremendously precious substance, and one as thaumaturgic as all the saints in the calendar. On the day when you are most discomfited, you will open this dish and eat these pills, in accordance with the directions on a manuscript in which you will find them wrapped. After which, all fear will take flight from your head; and in the midst of the worst of dangers, you will be like the most pious of cenobites amid the temptations of this world."

M. de Fierce, the dish in his hands, was silent.

"Who will assure me," he then timidly inquired, "that these globules or pills are not, instead, some virulent poison which my enemies have sent to me at your hands?"

"And who, pray," judiciously replied the giver of spells, "would have any motive in wishing the death of such a gentleman as you are, very ordinary in every respect and, what is worse, in bad standing at court?"

For this, the chevalier had no reply. Still, however inclined to libertinism he may have been, his mind rebelled at accepting, at their face-value, the words of a sorcerer in a green costume, with dress-sword and well-powdered wig.

"May I know, at least," he persisted, "the name of this drug, so fertile in miracles?"

"No," was the frank response. "For that name is by no means devoid of dread and mystery. However, to strengthen your courage, I will tell you that distant peoples, and those most abounding in knowledge and in wisdom, such as the Chinese, Tartars, Mongols and Malays, take care to make a daily use of this potent drug, which is the unfailing source of their rarest virtues. And truth obliges me to confess that I am not the inventor of it. This dish was filled long ago, at Nanking, an illustrious city of China; and it was the Venetian traveler, Marco Polo, a personal friend of mine, who made me a present of it."

"Do my ears deceive me?" queried the chevalier, surprised. "I imagined that old Venetian to have been dead for three or four centuries."

"For four-hundred-fourteen years, to be exact. But it may be, I am older than you think," replied the strange marquis, with a bow.

And he began to laugh,—a sepulchral laugh, which seemed to come from beyond the tomb. This laugh completed M. de Fierce's dismay. The chevalier fell back a number of paces.

"Sir," he said, "to please you, I am willing to accept as gospel truth all the incredible things which you have told me. But in return for that, I implore you to reveal to me your true identity and the mysterious manner in which you come to know all my secrets, you whom I look upon today for the first time."

Once more, the marquis-sorcerer burst into a loud laugh.

"That is the great mystery of mysteries itself which you are asking for now," he said. "It is impossible for me to satisfy your curiosity. Moreover, I told you but a while ago that I have no name; and that, I fancy, has been enough to frighten such a mind as yours. I retract, then. It is the truth that they call me the Marquis de Montferrat and Comte de Bel-lamye when I am in Venice, and the Marquis de Bet-mar, sometimes, when I am on my Portuguese cousin's estate. All these titles are mine, as rightly as earthly titles may be the patrimony of minds which are above the earth. It even has happened to me to be, in Spain, the Jesuit Aymar, along with all the trappings of his order. In Alsace, on the contrary, I was a Jew for a period of six months, and it was no jest, either. My name was Wolff then. Aix in Savoy looks upon me as Italian, and calls me Rotondo. Before that, I had the honor of being the confident of numerous princes, among whom you will be surprised, no doubt, to hear me mention Charles II. of Spain, Charles XII. of Sweden and Francis I. of France; for their majesties are today with the snows of yesteryear, and I alone am left.

"My French name? In three years, not any longer than that, I shall be famous in this court under the duly authenticated title of the Comte de Saint-Germain, and I, gladly, shall employ the weight of my reputation to be of service to you. My birth? Learned men will tell you that it is a royal one, and that a princess, traveling from Germany to Castille in quest of her crown, conceived me en route, through the workings of a certain pure and mysterious spirit. They are by no means wrong; although others, very sensibly, might allege my great age, which makes me by several centuries the elder of the queen, my mother. It does not matter; all that is a rebus scarcely worth engaging your perspicacity. Have no concern as to that; preserve the dish; learn how to make use of it; and may God, the master of men and of charms, keep you, even as I beseech him to do. Amen."

Saying this, the fabulous individual stood erect, rounded the end of the lane and disappeared.

* * *

M. Desherbiers, Marquis de PEstanduere and commander of the King's squadron, was not a courtier. His past career had been upon the various seas of the temperate and the tropical zone; and while he had acquired there a long wartime and maritime experience, as well as a certain reputation of which he might be proud, Versailles had remained for him an unknown land, regal and mysterious, out of which nothing could come that was not excellent and beyond compare. As a result, the Chevalier de Fierce was honored with a marvelous reception at Roche-fort. M. de PEstanduere immediately conferred upon him the title of my friend, and conducted him, with great ceremony, aboard the finest frigate of the fleet.

"Her name is La Menteuse" announced the valorous commander of the fleet, "and as a matter of fact, she frequently betrays, in a lying fashion, the hopes of the King's enemies, who find that their pursuit of her is vain. Your own valor, Monsieur le Chevalier, will find upon this splendid rover opportunity to achieve a profitable renown. I am aware that you are a novice at our trade; His Majesty has done me the honor to advise me of that fact. But I have taken care to provide you with excellent lieutenants, as well as with a boatswain whose humble birth alone has kept him in the lower ranks. The latter's name is Kerdoncuff; he is a full-blooded native of Cor-nouailles, and I shall introduce him to you, if you will permit me. In this manner, you will be spared all worry. What is more, we shall not get under way before a fortnight, and a fortnight is exactly the time required to transform a gentleman of your worth into an old sea-wolf."

The Menteuse was a noble frigate, carrying twenty-six cannons, the handsomest and the best constructed that were ever seen. But M. de Fierce, who was not extremely sensitive to martial beauties, paused merely long enough, in the ship's great well-lighted broadsides, to have a look at the double row of bronze artillery-pieces, squat and sinister, shooting toward the embrasures their wicked jaws, and ready to belch forth fire and steel.

* * *

However, under the conduct of the valiant Kerdoncuff, M. de Fierce stumbled his way through all the sections of his ship. Sufficiently apt at understanding and retaining a thing, he soon was able to distinguish the four masts,—the mizzenmast, the mainmast, the foresail and the bowsprit,—and was wonderfully well at home with the mizzen-topgal-lantsail, the topgallant and the royal, each of which is quite a different yard. He learned, also, that the figurehead supports the cutwater, the latter being a prolongation of the forecastle. He came to know, finally, that the quarter-board overlooked the quarter-deck, and that the great en-sign was struck at the gaff. But he flatly refused ever to go down into the gunroom.

"These great lords," grumbled Kerdoncuff, "are always afraid of putting themselves out by tarring their laces and other what-you-may-call-them gim-cracks, down in the powder-room."

M. de Fierce learned many other things. In the company of his chief and the captains, who frequently met at mess, he acquired the knowledge that maritime warfare is extraordinarily fertile in grapeshot and cannonadings, grapplings, shipwrecks,

massacres, drownings and slayings of all sorts. Terrible tales
flew back and forth, from one end of the mess-table to the other,
in the course of which, cups were incessantly emptied to the
King's health. Among those who took part in this drinking and
conversation were the MM. de Chaffault, de Fromentiere and
d'Amblimont, as well as the Comte Duguay and the Seigneur de
la Bedoyere, who afterwards distinguished himself greatly. But
distinguished among all was the Marquis de Vaudreuil, for whom
the chief displayed an especial fondness, and who was one of the
boldest sailors of his day.

In such company as this, M. de Fierce cut a small figure, his
courtly anecdotes raising him but little in the general esteem.
He nevertheless did his best to rise to the level of these men,
who daily throve on deeds of valor; but he did not succeed
very well. At the very first mess, he told of the feelings which
Madame de Cossac had had for him, and shamelessly took to
himself the credit for the sword-thrust with which his brother had
slain the marquis. But the exploit was coolly received by these
gentlemen, all of whom could count among their assets many
deeds of gallantry and many duels as well, and all of whom, on a
number of occasions, had put beneath the sod more redoubtable
champions than an old cuckold of a courtier.

But as for the tales of battles, surprise attacks and nocturnal
massacres, in which M. de PEstanduere's captains took particular
delight, the Chevalier de Fierce knew nothing of all this, and did
not venture to try out his imagination in the presence of auditors
so experienced as these.

Sometimes, indeed, in the course of the finest of these epic
narratives, on the part of the Marquis de Vaudreuil or oi M.
d'Amblimont, M. de Fierce would forget himself and tremble
visibly.

"That fop from Versailles," the chief finally confessed, "is
not, it may be, the gallant fellow that I took him to be."

The city of Rochefort was filled with merriment. The fleet's departure, which drew nearer hour by hour, filled the streets with a joyous tumult and with light-hearted revelry. Many were leaving who would not come back; and desiring to take with them to their deaths as many pleasant memories as possible, all vied with one another in drinking by the tumblerful, in singing songs at the top of their voices, and in rapturously caressing the women folk. M. de Fierce, though highly inclined to such amusements as these, took little part in them, his nights being so beset by fear that, as a result, he fell ill and pined away.

A few days afterward, matters grew worse still. The fleet weighed anchor, descended the Charente River and put out to sea. The task in hand was to escort, as far as the Windward Islands, a considerable convoy, one of a hundred-seventy merchant sails. M. de l'Estanduere had under his command, for this purpose, eight men of war, accompanied by four frigates, one of which was The Menteuse. As for the chevalier, as soon as the shoreline had faded from view, he ceased to live.

The imminent reality of danger came as a rude shock, after the long and terrible apprehensions which had gone before. M. de Fierce, completely done in, feigned seasickness, in order not to be compelled to put in an appearance. Old Kerdoncuff steered the Menteuse, while the chevalier, properly provided with drugs and decoctions, remained shut up in distress in the captain's cabin, reclining upon a very handsome rattan deck chair which had come from Pondichery.

From the second day on, this cabin, although a large light one, became for M. de Fierce a worse place to live in than the most baneful of the nine circles of Hell. In addition to his real sufferings, each hour of the day brought its special terror to the unfortunate captain. Before sunrise, it was the resounding morning-gun, signalling to sailors, recruits and deckhands the command to take down their swings or hammocks. From his rattan couch, M. de Fierce would fancy that he could hear the fire-drum, summoning each and every one to his post of battle. Later, it was the royal standards being ceremoniously reared at the poop, the soldiers of the guard saluting with a salvo from their muskets, which brought the luckless chevalier to his feet, in the firm belief that the English already were boarding them. After that, each skirmish-call or cannon-signal terrified him more and more; and when night came, no rest came with it, for the sailors, done with the labors of the day, would find recreation in singing songs in the prow, and their songs were all of a warlike character. The words, very distinct on the calm air, were audible in the poop:

—Vir' lof pour lof au meme instant, Nous l'attaqudmes par son avant A coups de z'haches d'abordage, De piques et de mousquetons! Nous la foutim'z a la raison.

Buvons un coup, buvons-en deux A la sante des amoureux! A la sante du Roy de France! Etm ... pour le Roy d'Angleterre Qui nous a declare la guerre. (*)

(Translator's Note)

*—Then tack for windward, sailor, tack: That's how we grappled her on her back, As with our hatchets we boarded her; Our pikes and muskets the story tell, How we swived her to a fare-you-welll

Then, drink up a cup, and drink up two, To the health of all good lovers true! And a health for the King of France I And a fig for the King of England, for 'Twas he who declared this wicked war.

The last lines were bawled out, at the top of their voices, by all of the feverish crew. The word guerre would fall with a savage sound upon the calm night air. And M. de Fierce, startled in his nightmare-haunted slumbers, would see himself now drowned, now hanged, and sometimes both at once.

Then, in the paroxysm of his fear, the chevalier would seize the dish with the miraculous pills and gaze upon it anguishedly, as upon the one talisman supremely capable of expelling the spectre of death from his mind.

* * *

Then came, one clear autumn day, as the sea-breeze was sweeping the blue sky, the famous 14th of October, 1747, which fell upon a Saturday.

At the first break of day, the brave Kerdoncufif, in great haste, entered the cabin where the chevalier lay tossing. A number of sails had been sighted to leeward, and the Tonnant, which was the name of the admiral's flagship, had signaled the frigates to run full sail ahead and reconnoiter the enemy.

M. de Fierce barely was able to murmur "run. . . . ahead,"— and then, his heart failed him completely.

The tumult, however, and the bustle and hustle of the fight restored him to his senses. And then, as he ransacked his pockets for his salts, his hand came into contact with the dish, which he always carried upon his person. And reflecting that there never would be a better occasion, he opened it.

Nine pills, each the size of a chick-pea, were there wrapped in silk-paper. As the paper was undone, they rolled out. They were a dull black, very like little pellets of resin or of pitch. They gave off no odor, and there appeared to be nothing in the least mysterious about them. To tell the truth, it seemed highly unreasonable to hope that a sovereign talisman would be found enclosed in that little blackish heap, which the wind from a fan might have caused to go flying out of the open portholes.

Nevertheless, the chevalier proceeded to read the manuscript directions contained in the silk-paper. The style was antiquated and the ink yellow.

"The nine pills herein contained are composed of a pure Chinese drug, mixed merely with precious spices, which consummate and multiply the virtues of the aforesaid drug. The first three which are swallowed, in the name of God, confer sapience and clarity of mind, in such a manner that ye shall be at once the like of Socrates, Lycurgus or Pythagoras. The three following ones, swallowed after the same fashion, imbue with courage, or a contempt for Old Death, in such a manner that ye shall be at once braver than Caesar, Hannibal or Judas Macca-baeus. And the seventh, eighth and ninth are the fatal dose, which a man is not to essay without having shrived himself, but which at once elevate him to the side of our Lord, and into the company of such saints and heroes as were Elijah, Hercules and John the Baptist. May God be with you."

"I may as well," thought the chevalier, "try the first three, even though I cannot quite clearly see how, in this melee, they are going to be of any use in driving away fear."

And he swallowed three of the pills, finding them more bitter than rose-root.

* * *

Swiftly as a gull, the Menteuse, all sails set, distanced her companions, in a headlong race to be the first to meet up with the enemy.

One after another, the sails which had been sighted took body above the watery horizon. Both frigates and men of war were to be made out, distinguishable by their difference in size, as well as by the differing number of their white-painted batteries. From

the top of a foremast, the lookout signaled that a large ensign had
been descried. There was no doubt, then, that this was the Vice-
Admiral of England's ship, and there was need of notifying the
commodore of this fact at once.

Old Kerdoncuff went to lay the matter before the captain.

M. de Fierce was still lying upon his rattan chair. He spoke in
a voice that was very calm, but low-pitched and slow:

"I wish to make good use of my eyes, and not to be disturbed.
Have them carry my chair to the quarterdeck."

For the first time, the crew had a sight of their captain. They
liked his face, although they found it a trifle pale; and they liked,
also, his appropriately resolute air.

"You mean to tell me," M. de Fierce was inquiring, "that
those ships will not be able to bombard us at a distance of less
than a mile? Lie aboard, then, and signal the fcmeraude to tack
about and warn the Tonnant. ... I count, do I not, fourteen ships
and five frigates? Signal the timeraude that I can see, behind
them.. . . That is all right. It is up to us to keep the English in the
dark as to our plans. Luff a little, men, as though we were going
to skirt them. . . ."

The English ships, making for windward, proceeded to lay
aboard; they were worried by the Men-teuse, and feared a trap.
At a distance, M. de l'Es-tanduere was occupied in tacking his
convoy about, which began putting off to starboard, giving the
enemy its back. Aboard the Menteuse, the grenadiers, up in the
ship's top, scenting what was up, were singing merrily:

> ... A la sante du Roy de France! Et m ... pour le Roy
> d'Angleterre.. ..

M. de Fierce interrupted this chantey:

"Tack about!" he cried.

With a surprising foresight, he had caught the enemy's
manoeuvre, and had anticipated it. Quicker than the big ships,—
which finally perceived what was doing,—the frigate made for

starboard and, before the English admiral had assembled his
fleet, was out of the enemy's reach by a good sea-mile.

"The nobility," mumbled old Kerdoncuflf, wagging his head,
"surely know many things which they have never learned. This
gentleman here who, all his life before, never left dry land, has
just completed a double manoeuvre that I should never have been
able to manage."

The French men-of-war were still to the windward, a few
leagues distant. In order to come up with them, it was necessary
for the English fleet to close in as compactly as possible and thus
lose long hours. Saving some unforeseen circumstance, such as
the springing up of a breeze, a storm or a dead calm, the convoy,
from this moment, was out of danger. It made off steadily, full
sail ahead. M. de Fierce could descry a member of the fleet
dropping oflf as a rear-guard, to cover the merchantmen's retreat.
The frigates spread out in its wake, while the rest of the fleet,—
namely, M. de PEstanduere, with seven men-of-war,—drew up
in battle-formation. The English ran along freely, trusting in their
fourteen sails. The result was, they fetched up in great disorder.
The Menteuse, gaining in speed, rounded the Tonnant, within
hailing distance.

"Thanks, Monsieur de Fierce," shouted the commodore; "the
late Comte de Tourville could not have done any better."

A singular smile illuminated the chevalier's face. The
helmsmen near the deck-chair observed their leader curiously.

His appearance was the same as usual, that of a sick man,—
excepting that his eyes, having lost their fleeting vivacity, had
taken on certain mysterious depths, along with a perturbing
fixity.

The battle began to leeward. It must have been midday. In
the ardor of the attack, the English vessels did not come up all
at once, but one after another; so that the best sailers, arriving
considerably in advance of the others, received a terrible
bombardment, the French artillery making use of them as targets.

Two sixty-cannon boats, having been badly dealt with, were compelled to take the wind and flee as quickly as possible. It was learned later that one of these was named the Lion and the other Princess Louisa.

"That's good enough!" remarked old Kerdoncuff, who had mounted the poop.

"Wait," was M. de Fierce's only comment, as he lay stretched out, his head in a cushion of Chinese silk.

The bulk of the English now had overtaken the French rear-guard, and proceeded to put up, in turn, so furious a fight that the next-to-last ship, despairing of victory, broke away from the fleet and surrendered. It was a mere fifty-six hull, too light for so savage a test as this. The end consort closed in to fill up the breach, and the battle continued.

"I must say," spoke up the boatswain, admiringly, "that M. de PEstanduere, is defending himself handsomely."

"It will be our turn soon," replied M. de Fierce. "Have them heave her to; we are too far out of the fight here."

The helmsmen threw all their weight upon the wheel;—and even as they did so, they caught sight of the captain opening a delft-ware sweetmeat-box, and saw him take from it three black comfits, which he swallowed.

* * *

Far away, to windward,—their hulls already having dropped below the horizon,—the convoy was still in flight. To leeward, barely "three ranges off, the English, furious with rage, were making a vain but stubborn effort against the commodore, who struggled on, unvanquished, at the head of his fleet.

Of his seven ships, three had given in, yielding to weight of numbers,—the Severn, the Fougueux and the Monarque;—but four kept on fighting,— the Tonnant, under the command of M. du Chaffault; the Terrible, with the Comte Duguay at its head; the Trident, whose deck was walked by the Chevalier d'Amblimont; and the Intrepide, aboard which the Marquis de Vaudreuil was engaged in distinguishing himself. Surrounded by enemies, these four noble ships heroically sustained their reputation, continuing to interrupt pursuit on the part of the English admiral, who was all prepared to hurl himself in the wake of the fleeing convoy. The sun, bespattered with blood and battle, was hastening toward the horizon, saddened at having to light the inevitable defeat of a handful of brave men, overwhelmed by a foe that outnumbered them. The dusk of evening rose in the east.

Another hour slipped by. Sea and sky had darkened as, around the proud phalanx, the cannon continued to thunder. But the flagship was no more to be seen, having parted with her four masts. Five of the enemy threw themselves upon this glorious ruin.

The Menteuse, still heaving to, was swaying lightly over the waves, her tall sails crackling occasionally with a mocking sound.

"Bear down upon the enemy!" suddenly commanded the Chevalier de Feirce.

"Your Lordship will excuse me," ventured the brave Kerdoncuflf, "but a frigate's place is not within range of the men-of-war. . . ."

"Where the King's honor is concerned," stated the captain, severely, "there are no longer either men-of-war or frigates. No man is at his post, if he has not an enemy on every hand."

This was uttered with an air of haughty nobility. M. de Fierce still lay in the hollow of his rattan chair. But by the last gleams of twilight, the boatswain could discern, crudely outlined against the brown pillow, a terrible face, shriveled with heroism, in which shone two sparkling eyes.

And the Menteuse, obediently, all sails set, darted to the fray.

* * *

It was past seven o'clock. Out of commission, but still obstinately battling for its honor, the Tonnant was scarcely able to answer the enemy's fire any longer. Its companions, sacrificing their own safety to that of their admiral, were concerned solely with bringing aid to the latter.

The Comte Duguay had been the first to attempt this. Whirling audaciously, wind ahead, he had come up to the commodore, and had prepared, while covering the admiral with his broadsides, to cast him a tow-line. M. d'Amblimont, jealously eager for the same honor, imitated without delay the manoeuvre of his consort. For an instant, victory appeared to smile upon the two of them. The men-of-war drifted in between the lines, bravely employing their last bullets in one final bombardment. And then, suddenly, the rigging, literally chopped to bits like mincemeat, broke and vanished with the breath of evening, and the day, indeed, was lost. Disabled, shattered and surrounded on all sides, the Terrible and the Trident succumbed to overpowering numbers. And yielding to dolorous destiny, the MM. Duguay and d'Amblimont hauled down their fleur-de-lis, the daylight streaming through the rents of the glorious lace open-work.—The Intrepide alone remained beside the Tonnant.

As a last hope, M. de Vaudreuil's masts were still standing. But the Tonnant was no longer anything more than a blood-drenched deck, where the captain and his standards lay in one vast confusion,—a disorder so complete that a mere cadet, a Knight of Malta, was now in command of the crew. His name was Suffren; and weeping with rage, he obstinately refused to surrender the ship.

And now, blindly faithful to his duty, the Marquis de Vaudreuil proceeded to tack about,—hopelessly,— as the MM. Duguay and d'Amblimont had done. But at this point, fickle fortune took a turn; for at this very moment, a frigate was to be seen leaping suddenly out of the darkness and hurling itself, blindly, into the melee.

A voice, exceedingly calm and miraculously distinct, rose above the cannon. It was M. de Fierce giving his orders, as calmly as though he had been on dress-parade. The tow-lines

of the Intrepide were laid hold of by the Menteuse, and amid
a hurricane of bullets, the disdainful frigate bore the extended
cables to the Tonnant.

"Long live the King!" shouted the Marquis de l*Estanduere.
"Monsieur le chevalier, you have saved our honor!"

The English, stupefied, saw the two ships put out, while the
frigate, insanely audacious, stayed to cover their retreat.

For the course of a minute, the firing ceased, as the
disconcerted enemy collected their wits, their eyes endeavoring
all the while to pierce the cloud of smoke which added to the
blackness of the night. Aboard the Menteuse, the dead and dying
were being cared for.

"Really," remarked M. de Fierce, "I believe that I am
wounded. Does there happen to be a surgeon still alive?"

There was none. But the helmsmen brought a lantern, and the
chevalier was enabled to make out that he was, truly, wounded. A
bar-shot had fractured both his legs, and the blood was streaming
in wide rivulets from the double wound.

"Pooh!" said the wounded man, with a smile, "there is
no longer any need of surgical assistance. That fellow Saint-
Germain's talisman obviously is not effective against cast-iron
and steel shells. But no difference; seeing I have reached this
point, I may, without danger, swallow those last pills. . . ."

He swallowed them, smiled once more,—a melancholy
smile—and tossed the dish into the sea.

At that very moment, the English ships began their
manoeuvres. Ignoring the frigate, they gave chase to the Tonnant
and the Infrepide. The truth is, the fight had been a hot one
for them, and many of them were drifting about in winded
fashion, without any lively yearning for fresh hazards. Only the
Devonshire, which was the flagship, and the Nottingham, under
command of Sir Philp Saumarez, succeeded in catching up with
M. de l'Estanduere. The Tonnant was incapable of any further
effort, and they were two against one.

The Devonshire herself had suffered at the hands of the French and now manoeuvred with care, giving up the fight after a few last broadsides. But the Nottingham, which had escaped lightly up to now, soon out-manoeuvred the Intrepide. All was lost now, it seemed; but M. de Vaudreuil, knowing the Menteuse from past experience, by no means abandoned hope, as he cast a glance behind him in the direction of the frigate.

He was right in his reckoning. The Menteuse now cooly entered the fight. With an unheard-of audacity, the chevalier took up a position between the men-of-war, boldly leaving his infantile thirteen-piece broadsides exposed to the Nottingham's seventy cannons. This boundless courage on the part of the captain raised the enthusiasm of the remaining consorts to so high a pitch that, for a moment, victory was in doubt.

But a frigate confronting a ship of the line is like a bad boy facing a hardened warrior. The English soon recovered their self-possession, and the Menteuse, riddled from all sides, began to yield. The Intrepide, under shelter of its frail protector, effected repairs in great haste and reloaded its cannon. For in war, there is no slight distraction which may not, at the proper moment, take fortune by storm and change defeat into success.

In short, it would, perhaps, have been enough, had the Marquis de Vaudreuil felt like firing over the frigate. But the Menteuse had received, surely, its share of bullets that day.

"It would be a great pity," exclaimed the brave captain, "to finish off, like that, a valiant craft, to whose devotion on two occasions we, perhaps, owe our salvation."

M. de Fierce now understood the Marquis' hesitation. The three last pills were melting in his veins, conducting him effortlessly into the sublime battalion of martyrs and of demigods.

He gazed thoughtfully at the Nottingham, which had taken fresh courage, and at the Intrepide, whose bronze cannon with their black eyes returned his gaze,—eyes brimming with the mystery of death. And then, of a sudden, he shouted:

"Par la sambleu, Monsieur de Vaudreuil, why do you hesitate to fire across our carcass? Let them have a broadside! And long live the King!"

This was done, and so quickly that there seemed to be in it something of magic. The broadside came, battering at once the Nottingham and the Menteuse. The Englishman tumbled whatever way chance would have it, his rigging in shreds and three hundred corpses strewing his decks. And thus, protected by the smoke of bottle as the gods of Olympus were by the dense clouds which hid their flight, the Intrepide and the Tonnant escaped.

The Menteuse, pounded by a squall of steel, staggered at first like a dying beast, and then was swallowed up. The English were able to save only a few strays, and to collect two or three floating corpses. In this manner, they took from the sea the remains of the Chevalier de Fierce, whose heart a bullet had reached. Filled with admiration for so noble an enemy, Lord Hawke, Vice-Admiral of England, paid the chevalier full miltary honors, burying him in a fleur-de-lis flag,—the Menteuse's own ensign,—not dreaming, it is certain, that, all his lif e, this incomparable hero never had been any but the most arrant of cowards.

The Church

When I awoke, I understood at once: my watch showed thirteen minutes after nine. The church was closed. The Swiss had not seen me in my hiding-place, and I found myself a prisoner.

A prisoner. I opened my mouth to call out, then shrugged my shoulders. What was the use? No one would hear me. Outside, it was snowing. The square, surely, was deserted; and moreover, the walls were too thick. Besides, who would pay any attention to my cries?

No, there was nothing to do but wait, wait until they came to open the doors for early-morning mass, —wait and go back to sleep. A deuce of an idea, that of mine, to enter this damned church in order to get away for an hour from the biting wind of the streets! A deuce of an idea, above all, to take hiding inside this confessional, there to meditate on the furtive sins of the devout ones, slyly and blushingly confessed through the narrow grating, the thick veil and the dense half-night of the sanctuary. By great good luck, the nave was heated. With uncertain steps, I ventured in the direction of the hot-air pipe, knocking, here and there, against benches and chairs, for it was fearfully dark. At a distance, in the mysterious recess formed by the arches, a solitary red light burned, big as a star. A tremendous silence reigned, and each of my foot-steps awoke, at the top of the vault, a bizarre echo that was prolonged in a most unlikely manner.

Near the vestrymen's bench, I came upon a mildly warm and sufficiently comfortable corner. I spread my fur-lined pelisse over three faldstools, and lay down, rather well off than otherwise. Round about me, the chapels, pillars and shrines appeared to be mounting guard. Despite the strangeness of the place, I felt reassured and peaceful. My impression of absolute isolation was accompanied by one of utter security. The external world, now far off, became for me, in my somnolence, a peril that I had conjured away,—a peril of fog and ice, which the gentle warmth of the Gothic structure, its immense walls and closed doors, resolutely excluded. My eyes, used to the darkness, were barely able to make out, through the ancient panes, the pallid transparence of the snowy night. And no sound came to me, except, very dim and indistinct, the last clamor of belated tramways in the deserted city without. And so, I went back to sleep.

Now, this adventure occurred at Lyons, in the Church of St. John the Evangelist, the metropolitan cathedral, in the year of Grace one thousand-nine-hundred, on the seventh night of January.

* * *

I positively do not know what o'clock it may have been when I awoke for the second time. I wanted to look at my watch, but my match-box was empty. The red light which I had seen must have been hid from me by a pillar, for I could not see it any more.

And then, suddenly, in that utterly empty nave, my ear caught the sound of footfalls.

I do not know what form terror most commonly puts on with men. In books, one reads of hair standing on end, of cold sweats and convulsive tremors. I experienced nothing of the sort. And yet, I was so frightened that, for some seconds, I thought I should go mad. My whole brain reeled. Ideas swarmed, piecemeal, without succeeding in effecting a union in the form of whole ideas, so that I was unable even to imagine a cause,—natural or supernatural,—for the sound which I continued to hear. I could only remain there, wrapped in my pelisse, paralyzed, thunder-struck.

The terrifying footfalls traversed the whole of the nave, from the main door to the choir. There, they mounted the steps of the great altar, and I could not hear them any more as they went on across the carpet. But shortly afterward, they were audible again, muffled and distant. I knew that they were going around to the rear of the altar. And after the fresh silence,—with the carpet once more to cross,—I heard them redescending into the nave. They passed at a distance of ten meters from me, ten meters, and then died away lugubriously, being dully repeated by the shuddering echoes, all the way to the door, where they came to a standstill.

What was I to do? Arise and walk,—walk in the direction of this improbable being, which, at the stroke of midnight, would soar away into the spaces of the inaccessible cathedral? I would not have done that for a kingdom;—no, not for Richard III.'s horse! To say nothing, to keep quiet, without budging or breathing, without seeing or understanding what was going on, and to live thus,—no, to agonize thus,—for five, six, seven— how many?—hours? Physiologists assert that dreams—and, therefore, nightmares—of necessity begin and end the same second, no matter how complicated, how labyrinthine they may be. And yet which one of us, upon awaking from a terrifying dream, has not felt his reason tottering,—upon awaking from one of those same dreams which, yet, are not so long in duration as the tick of a pendulum? For me, there were twenty—there were thirty-thousand successive, uninterrupted nightmares that obstinately came to perch in my brain,—since there were all of thirty-thousand seconds separating me from the longed-for dawn.

And I knew, from evidence which I could not gainsay, that in the morning, the beadles would find in the nave, stretched out upon the vestrymen's bench, nothing more than a corpse, or better, a maniac, a bellowing, clawing madman, the whites of his eyes rolling upwards from their sockets. And so, crawling on all fours between the chairs, I crept indirectly toward the center of the church, turning pale at the idea of a bump, or a grating sound which would reveal my whereabouts. I crept thus all the way to the middle flagstones, which those foot-steps had just grazed. And I waited, with failing heart.

I waited long! The steps, apparently, were not of a mind to come. I could hear them distantly hammering the resounding pavement, to the right, to the left, at the back. Twice, they crossed the choir; I could hear the grating of the little marble door. Then, at one side of the nave, a chair fell, and this gave rise to a long weird sound, which—I do not know why—had something in it that was reassuring. But only for a minute; for fear choked me afresh as the steps approached. They finally took the central aisle of the nave, and I could feel my heart standing still in my bosom. Surely, at that instant, my life was not worth much; the least unexpected thing, the crackling of a twig, a gust of wind, and I should have been dead, dead of fright, nothing more or less. But no twig crackled, and no gust came. I beheld, instead, so near at hand that it even grazed me in passing, a great brown cloak, topped by a monk's hood, which at once melted away into the night.

No matter! I took a deep breath: I had seen it, and for the reason that I had seen it, it was already less terrible. Moreover, the thing had passed very close to me, without seeing me or divining my presence. That alone gave me an obvious advantage: of the two of us, it was I who was the better concealed, the more mysterious. Man or ghost, I could give him a hundred times the fear I had just experienced, merely by overturning a chair or bursting into a laugh that would go echoing through that majestic silence. As yet, however, I did not dare.

The unknown being had paused near the high altar. Once more, his footfalls died in the carpet of the steps. Immediately, a light began to dance near the tabernacle. A pair of candles were lighted. And in the little zone of light, I could see the brown cloak once more. The hood had been tossed back, and I could dimly make out a man's long, backward-flowing hair.

Then, the vision stretched out its arms, and the cloak fell
to the floor. Against the white altar, a tall, slender body was
now outlined, clad in an outlandish sort of black gold-braided
uniform, with a sword at its side. I could distinguish the sword
clearly enough, for at that moment, the stranger unsheathed it,
and the flame of the candles played over its naked blade. It was
a lightly curved sword, almost a saber, with a gilded handle. The
man placed it upon the altar, then unclasped the sheath, which
fell to the steps with the sound of clinking metal.

I beheld, then, a very singular sight.

The black gold-braided stranger departed from the high-altar
and disappeared at the left of the nave, returning a moment later,
bearing in his hands the red lamp which I had first glimpsed. This
lamp he placed upon the tabernacle, between the two candles, the
whole being done silently, without any hesitation or groping. The
stranger was evidently familiar with every nook of the cathedral,
and as able to find his way about in the darkness as he would
have been in broad daylight. Extending his hand above the lamp,
he remained motionless for a number of minutes, as though he
were deliberately burning his fingers. And I could hear, in the
unbroken silence, a recurrent crackling, like that of a small fish
being fried. I took a better look. The black stranger's hand was
not in contact with the flame. He was holding, by the tips of his
fingers, a long needle, dipping it at intervals into a small flagon
which I had not noticed at first. It was the needle which was
doing the crackling, above the red lamp; the needle and the drops
of some strange substance which were being cooked thus, one
after another. Heavy smoke-spirals were now rising and falling in
front of the altar, and an uncanny odor, one I never had smelled
before, thin and potent, reached my nostrils. This lasted for two,
three minutes. Then, with a slow and solemn gesture, the stranger
brought his fingers to his mouth and appeared to be swallowing
the ashes of this mysterious perfume of his.

Troubled thoughts wavered within me, thoughts of defilement and of sacrilege, of the black mass and of magic spells. But no, the golden gate of the tabernacle remained closed, while the stranger displayed on the whole, an obvious respect for the holy place. Twice, I saw him go up and come down the steps, making, with a sweeping gesture, the sign of the cross upon his bosom. This man was a Christian and a Catholic, used to churches; and once assured of this, I felt no more alarm. Did there exist, then, at the very heart of my own modern and liberal creed, certain esoteric cults whose priests, clad in black and gold and bearing curved swords, were in the habit of performing their dark offices far from the eyes of the faithful, in the nocturnal solitude of cathedrals? At that very moment, were other like priests, in other churches, engaged in celebrating identical rites? This same strange incense undoubtedly burned above other liturgic lamps, dispersing its disturbing aroma through many an empty nave. Up to the eucharistic moment, when these sword-bearing priests, lifting in their fingers the incense scattered by the flame, swallowed it like a Host. . . .

I was no longer afraid, no longer afraid of anything. But a growing uneasiness took possession of my nerves. Too many alarming suspicions were besieging my brain. And more strongly, from moment to moment, the temptation laid hold of me to break the spell of silence and of mystery, which I felt was strangling me. The movement I had imagined myself making, a while back,—the chair noisily overturned upon the pavement,—my fingers now toyed with the idea, being stealthily attracted by the back of the nearest prie-dieu. I was haunted by an obsession for uproar and tumult.

I suddenly succumbed to it. With all my strength, I wrenched the prie-dieu from the floor and sent it hurtling toward the roof. It came down, somewhere or other, with a sort of terrifying detonation which was endlessly taken up by all the bellowing echoes. I waited, weak with anxiety and longing, for a sudden and atrocious terror to manifest itself in the person of the other, the stranger down there, who as yet had exhibited no signs of fear. My eager eyes rested intently upon the somber upright figure at the foot of the altar.

But he did not stir. He merely turned, nonchalantly, to scrutinize the dark church. For a second; and then, I heard him laugh,—a short, disdainful laugh,—laugh as he turned away. And the terror which I had cast at him now gushed up vigorously in my own heart, rebounded by the intrepid substance of this stranger's being. What manner of man was this, and what sacrilege was it,—a sacrilege, possibly, connected with that fantastic incense of his,—that reared him so high above mortal men?

Thereupon, what reason remained to me began to dance and waver, like the two candles of the altar. Completely overwhelmed and battered down, without the will either to cry out or to keep silent, I found time, space and life itself becoming for me vague notions, of which I ceased any longer to be conscious. Not fainting, but utterly befuddled, I beheld, as in a dream-mist, the black and gold stranger carrying the liturgic lamp back to I knew not where; and then, I saw him girding on his sword and hooking the clasps of his cloak about him once more. I perceived—on, I guessed—that he was coming down the steps of the altar, and I could hear his footfall upon the flagstones, without being altogether certain that this was not, simply, the echo of his former footsteps, now reaching my ears for the first time. I could hear the creaking of a door and the crunching of wooden stairs. Lastly, and this was my last sensation on that hypnotic night, I became aware of his dark presence high up in the pulpit, his frock trailing down over the velvet baluster. The candles, burnt to the ends, flickered and became extinct, restoring to the depths of the nave a darkness that was less dreadful. . . .

* * *

Sleep, lethargy, half-death? I do not know. The dull dawn, more pallid than a being of snow, mournfully lighted up the windows of the church. Keys v-grated in locks, a door opened and sacristans moved about, without seeing me, without seeing us. For he was there, still. The Gothic walls had not opened to provide a miraculous escape for him. I could hear him coming down from the pulpit, and I recognized his rhythmed footfall echoing under the sonorous roof. He did not hide himself. He walked to the door, without haste. And I tremulously brushed him, just sufficiently to be able to feel, in reality, the sheath of his sword under his flowing cloak. He paused under the portal, facing the square white with snow. And I could see his face, which was somehow human, and his eyes,—eyes that were very fixed, and whose gaze did not meet mine.

Then, he very simply went away, and was at once swallowed up in the snow.

The Vermin

The palace of Tong-Doc is on the edge of the City. The City is a Far-Eastern capital, a mongrel capital, Mongolian and Malay. A lank and brown people there bend under the barbarous yoke of white faces come from the west.

Tong-Doc's palace, however, is not one of those lumpish structures, bristling with turrets or grated with colonnades, after the fashion of conquerors. The old prince, a servile traitor, has cast to the dogs his honor as a patriot and his loyalty as a subject,—has cast to the dogs that ancestral cult which lends color to his sceptic philosophy;—has openly proclaimed himself a European, a democrat and a Catholic;— but has preserved, not without a number of polite excuses, his sympathy for his race's distinctive art. Tong-Doc's palace is a park, rendered somber by great cedars, where slumber five scattered yamens, widened by vast terraces. The rafters are of marble and the partitions of ebony, while the roofs are of varnished porcelain. Everywhere, there is a profusion of inlaid mother-of-pearl. The water gushes joyously under the trees; the wind brings its coolness to the depths of the inmost courts; while the sun never once has trespassed, even on the verandas.

In the yamen which is reserved for her personal use,—under the rhythmic wing-beats of white-silk pankas,—Tong-Doc's daughter, who in the olden days would have been a princess, is taking her noonday siesta.

* * *

No one ever has called her by her true name,—that perilous name which is, yet, murmured each evening, with regret and with desire, in the dark canhas of the rice-field. True to the pliant policy he has adopted, Tong-Doc calls her Anna, like a child of Europe. She is Anna, likewise, to the gay bevy of lieutenants and naval ensigns, who frequently come to the Palace to play tennis with Tong-Doc's daughter, and to receive, afterward, from her little brown hand, a cup of tea, sugared after the English manner, along with cream and cakes. Mademoiselle Anna smiles and drops a curtsy,—they have educated her in a convent; Mademoiselle Anna plays admirable tennis with her partner, the young wife of the vice-resident; Mademoiselle Anna professes a certain contempt for Yunnan tea,—an infusion of warm water, but dear! Mademoiselle Anna, lastly, flirts—flirts a great deal, and with so knowing a degree of coquettishness that two of the governor's aides-de-camp are beginning, it is said, to be a bit unnerved by the pastime. All in all, Mademoiselle Anna differs very little from any "Mademoiselle Anna" of Paris or of London; and yet, one would make a mistake in overlooking the oriental costume, the sober sheath of black silk, buckled with gold, and the Annamite sandals, revealing an irreproachable Asiatic foot,—in overlooking, above all, the differing type of beauty, finer and less lurid, more deeply rooted in race,—mysterious.—But it does not matter; Tong-Doc's daughter really has forgotten her race and her destiny that is no more. She is not familiar with the old language of the Empire, and when she speaks of those who were her vassals, she says: "the natives."

* * *

It is four o'clock. Today, they are not playing tennis. But two white-mustached colonels have come to pay Tong-Doc a friendly visit. Mademoiselle Anna gives her orders: tea will not be served.

How is that, Mademoiselle! You are not going to give us alcohol?"

"Oh, a very little, Colonel! It is a cocktail I thought up myself. You take a finger of maraschino, a drop of Scotch whiskey . . ."

"And a lot of ice?"

"And heaps of ice! Whole icebergs. Floes of it! Trust me, Colonel."

The fivefold-laced kepis shake in a gale of laughter —under the ancient and unremembering cedars.

* * *

It is five o'clock, the excursion-hour. Clad in a heavily embroidered green robe,—never yellow, never purple, never the proscribed imperial colors!—Tong-Doc's daughter climbs into a victoria for her evening drive. The victoria is a "Binder," and the horses are two Australians, of that superb breed which lives but a year under the sun of Indo-China. In all the city, there is no turnout that is more elegant, more Parisian. The livery is a restrained one, without cockades, while the black varnish knows no armorial bearings of any sort.

The fashionable drive is a park-lane, half a league long, a straight path covered with red sand. Along this path, Asiatic Nature displays her melancholy splendors: rice-fields green as lawns, shrubbery-muffled rivulets, tall thickets of graceful bamboo, forests of hardy cabbage-palms. And the sun, fatal to European skulls, embroiders with rubies and emeralds all the shimmering substance of this humid greenery. For centuries, literate Emperors, invisible behind the curtains of their pure-gold palanquins, have aired their disdainful indolence amid these preferred shades.

Tong-Doc's victoria mingles with the other victorias along the drive. There are two lines of carriages, going up and coming down the lane, with high-stepping steeds. The light-colored habits, the gay umbrellas, the nude half-gloved white arms,— and the sun at the horizon's edge, grown less brutal with its declining rays,—all this is a glimpse of Europe, a sumptuous glimpse of Armenonville or Hyde Park.—The green robe, embroidered with hieratic leaf-work,—tone laid over tone,— barely makes a discreetly exotic splash;—barely: Mademoiselle

Anna sits negligently under her parasol and casts mocking glances at the assiduous cavaliers who greet her in passing! Here and there, hands move, and good-evenings are exchanged on the wing, in the cool tones of young girls' voices. The evening is already hastening on, streaking with brown the sinking coat of buff, like a tiger's fur. The victorias speed back to the city; but by the gleam of coach-lanterns, belated ones are still able to make out the amused smile of Tong-Doc's daughter, who stays till the last,—an extremely distant smile, certainly, and one that has in it something of that everlasting sneer which is to be found, in the pagodas, on the grimacing faces of the Empire's forgotten idols.

* * *

Ten o'clock, the theatre-hour. The proscenium is banked with a harvest of roses. Tong-Doc's daughter, reclining, in a half-meditative mood, is listening to Samson. Her little mother-of-pearl opera-glasses occasionally skim the tenor or the contralto,—but more often, they search out the boxes and make minute note of the toilets to be glimpsed there.

In the glow of the lights, the slim, dull beauty of the noble Asiatic shines resplendently. The sumptuous robe tightly sheathes the hips of a woman and the figure of a fay; the proud, slender bust may be seen expanding the silk that covers it, while the delicate neck appears to be of some unknown metal, lighter-colored than bronze and more precious than silver. Slim, subtle hands, irreproachable arms and a face that remains enigmatic despite the cold, pure gleam of the eyes,—all this evokes the thought of some strange and ancient statue, modeled by a master who was in love with mystery and the unknown. Yet, over the atavistic mask of face, the novelty of education has laid a new mask; and smile, look and gesture concur in transforming the Very Distant Princess into an altogether modern Parisienne, ill-disguised under her Oriental robe.

At the door of the box, there are two discreet knocks. It is a visit from the commandant, a very young and flirtatious lieutenant-colonel. Compliments, bows, kissing of fingers. For the time, Saint-Saens has the worst of it. They sit down, make themselves comfortable and chatter on, the music forgotten,— just as it is at Paris.

* * *

And now, it is night,—a night heavy and scintil-lant, an Indo-Chinese night, warm as a summer's day. Tong-Doc's daughter has returned to her yamen. The enervated city is asleep. In the silent avenues, there is no longer any one to gaze upon the violet-colored row of electric bulbs, veiled by a curtain of green trees.

Only the opium-dens, bordering the dark arroyo, glow dimly red in the night. Dens of prostitution, above all. The low doors open into wretched, dimly lighted smoking-rooms, with a floor of trampled earth, walls of botched plaster, rafters caving in and rotting mats. Two large oil-lamps befoul the stale air. In the interior, four closed booths with flapping wickets give shelter to lubricious couples. On the floor, lamp, pipe and needle await the smoker. But there are no smokers; there come here only a few drunken sailors or, occasionally, some merrymaking crowd in a mood for low company.

Far away, behind Tong-Doc's palace, at the small postern where a sharpshooter stands sentinel,—flat beret firmly planted upon his correct topknot and musket resting against his right forearm,—light footfalls crunch the sand, and a door silently opens on its hinges. A brown figure has passed through, the figure of a woman slipping out of the palace. Yet the sentinel has seen nothing,—seen nothing, for he stands there mute and impassive, his attention solely fixed upon the shrubbery which borders the circular roadway.

* * *

At the end of the arroyo's quay, amid the low canhas, the remotest of the opium-dens opens its wan mouth. Three wrinkled prostitutes,—young or old, it would be hard to say,—are crouched beside an ambiguous lad; and from bumpers of rice-

brandy, the four of them are engaged in filling the cups without
handles. A teapot steams in the corner.

The worm-eaten door now opens, and some one comes in.
A woman, young and beautiful, very elegant-appearing in the
mean simplicity of her brown robe. And then, an altogether weird
thing happens. The prostitute and the giton, ordinarily lacking in
courtesy and slow to return greetings, hastily rise and join their
hands, in keeping with their bended heads,—which is the rite
of profound respect. Phrases are exchanged, phrases couched
in the purest Annam dialect,—the visitor giving her commands
in a few brief words, the hosts, meanwhile, stammering humble
professions of homage and offers of service. Quickly, the brandy
is put aside, the lamp is lighted and the pipe heated in its flame.
One of the prostitutes, upon her knees, proffers the first cup
of tea,—a green tea of Yunnan, of which the barbarians know
nothing,—and the opium, above the lamp, begins its mysterious
crackling.

* * *

But at this moment, the door opens with a hubbub, and a
noisy band bursts headlong in, a crazy band of merry-makers,
returning from a supper-party and looking for debauchery.
There are among them officers, functionaries, a magistrate,—
perfect picture of the invading Occident, the very essence of
Europe, stubbornly bent upon crushing out, under the heel of
its gross and busy barbarism, the indolent and subtle wisdom
of the vanquished Orient. All these riotous ones come bursting
clamorously into the canha, exclaiming loudly:

"How terrible!—What a stench!—Look, there's the brat I
was telling you of.—What sordid vice you find among these
savages!"

The woman visitor, stretched out beside the lamp, the
bamboo pipe in her frail hand, has not deigned to turn her head.

"It takes some nerve to lie down there!—And have a look at
the vermin, will you! They're swarming moderately thick this
evening."

"The vermin?"

"Yes, the cockroaches, the moths, the ants, the spiders, the millipeds, the scorpions, the what not. This is their kingdom; they're in full sway here. There are times when the mats are black with them."

"Ugh!"

"But look, who's that congai smoking over there? Upon my word, here's a pretty girl that I haven't seen."

Impassively, the smoker slowly draws in the black smoke, her engrossed eyes fixed on nothingness. Possibly, she does not understand. Women of the city, however, are rare who do not possess some small smattering of the language of their masters.

"Well, little one? Let us have a look at your nose."

The speaker is one of the leaders of his race, in point both of birth and of skill. Italian and French at the same time, poet, doctor and soldier, he is the harmonious embodiment of the refinement and wit of the two peoples, as well as of the pride and wisdom of three castes.

He is, for all of that, in the presence of the complex Far-East, like a child confronting a puzzle.

He has drawn near the smoker, and with his finger, he now touches her shoulder. She looks at him, coldly. A sense of strangeness deepens between them.

"She is pretty. What is your name?—So you haven't anything to say? She doesn't speak French; she's a little savage.—Come on, let's have a look at your breasts. . . . Oh, that's quite all right, in a case like this. . . . She'll do it, right enough. . . . Ah, no? No further than that? Have your own way, my dear. I suppose you know that you've a very pretty figure?"

"Ah, ha! I've just thought of it. Doesn't she impress you, old man, as being the very picture of Tong-Doc's daughter, Anna?"

"My word, there is a slight.. . . . But still, not quite so fine-featured, something more common about her."

"What do you expect here?"

"That's all right; she's a good deal above the average. And as for you, Baba, you're in luck! Who's your new boarder?"

Baba,—Annamite dialect,—old woman.

The oldest of the prostitutes laughs, her big obscene mouth split back over her black teeth,—laughs a brawling, stupid laugh, underneath which no one in the world would suspect that a fierce mockery lies concealed. And then, with jabbering words, she explains. The visitor arrived yesterday; she comes from down there,—an indeterminate place, a vague gesture; her name is Thi-Nam, a very common name— "at least, if you don't mind. ..."

"I don't mind. Is that *objet d'art* for sale?"

A mad laugh, growing more brawling and stupid. The three prostitutes bend double, writhing with mirth. No, such a thing cannot be; it is the most impossible thing in the world. Thi-Nam is inviolable, in the most literal sense of the word. Why? The captain would like to know? Ah, gods! because,—an obscene gesture,—for the reason, alas, that this beauteous angel is but a mangy lamb, very mangy. Thi-Nam is sick, and the worthy captain has but to insist a little in order to acquire, upon the spot, the most marvelous dose of syphilis in the whole country. Just so: those coral lips, those black eyes with the silver gleams, that throat, so proud and so pure,—all that is rotten!

"Ha! there's realism for you, old man!—Beware, after this, of little girls who have the air of being very good little girls.— This old witch has a frank enough way with her.—Pshaw, she's afraid the morals officers will be around.—And look at the little one, will you? It's all one to her, this public revelation! A white woman would die of shame; but the women here are like so many bitches. Pity the race!"

"Come on, there's nothing doing in this mudhole. Shall we go?"

They leave. The last of them, the Frenchman who is a son of Italy, pauses upon the threshold for a backward look. He has a dim intimation that there are many mysterious things between those four miry walls, many redoubtable enigmas behind those brown foreheads, which think other and different thoughts than the thoughts of the Occident. Nevertheless, he leaves, after a moment's hesitation. And no suspicion comes to him of the improbable truth of the matter.

* * *

As the door closes, there is a grinding of bolts in their sockets, and the erstwhile unaccommodating matron throws herself to her knees and touches her head to the mats.—The Holy Princess, Suzeraine of the City, the One Set Apart,—by right of race,— for the Imperial Couch, the daughter of Tong-Doc, who formerly was the seventh in the Empire, the Irreproachable Virgin, will she grant pardon, will she pardon the most worthless of her slaves, vile as the excrement of toads, the blasphemy which has been uttered? Will she show mercy to the criminal creature who, in order to ward off barbarian outrage, has dared defile her Princess with her, the slave's own, vile ignominy? The prostitutes and the giton tremble, their hands joined and their foreheads in the mud. Tears flow now. Gone the hypocritical grimace which serves to mock the oppressors' brutality; bitter tears are flowing now, hot with terror and with indignation.

Impassive, with the hieratic disdain of her ancestors resurrected in her eyes, Tong-Doc's daughter gazes upon her subjects and does not speak. Only an impatient clack of the tongue escapes her: the pipe is empty. Timidly, the women come to the rescue. And once again, the black fumes rise and fall in the silent smoking-room.

The magical odor expands and hovers. The mats become impregnated with it, then the earth of the floor, and the walk, and the rafters of the ceiling.

Mysteriously drawn, the numberless hordes of vermin fare forth, from every cranny and every hole, and make their way, little by little, toward the lamp.

For the kindly drug spreads its mantle of royalty to cover all beings. Nothing living is beyond reach of its scepter; and in the presence of those potent atoms with which it saturates the dens, the wood-louse's instinct sways like human reason,—that same reason which leads a fallen princess to come here to forget a throne that is no more,—to forget it in the midst of a population of insects, lifted for an hour above their lowly animality.

The vermin slowly converge towards the smoker, without daring to touch her body, which smells of opium. They are teeming all around. Between the mats, the interstices of brown earth cease to be visible, for the reason that the mats are now as brown as the earth, brown with vermin-heaps.

The carina is several generations old, and myriads of insects are pullulating in its worm-eaten planks,— myriads, also, in the damp, warm earthen floor. In the corners of the gaping roof, great hairy spiders have spun their webs. Along the bamboos which serve as beams, and between the crossed laths which comprise the ceiling, brown cockroaches toddle and sometimes clumsily drop from their perches. Others, very big and black, spread their lazy wings and precipitate themselves, in uncouth fashion, from one wall to the other, only to come tumbling down half dead from the impact. Down below is the realm of the ants, mill-moths, scorpions and earwigs; all run busily over the mats, chasing and evading each other, colliding and fighting, loving and devouring, in accordance with the laws of race and of sex. On the walls, little short lizards emerge from the plaster crevices and leap from one chink to another, with abrupt, timid stops. In the center of the room, finally, in the tepid, moldy atmosphere of the place, the mosquitoes, in increasing numbers, dance their sarabands, as they assail the oil-lamp, only to fall, one after another, into the flame.

And now, the black smoke is having its effect on all this confusion of furtive life-forms. Little by little, the buzzings and the cracklings die away. Not that the vermin have fallen asleep; but their troubled instincts have been diverted, as gleams of intelligence, —a calm and sanguine intelligence,—begin to see the light of day within their rudimentary brains.

The vermin now suspend their never abandoned movements. Long concentric lines hesitate and hover above the smoker, finally encircling her as with a motionless aureole. Taken by surprise at first, soon growing avid, their thin breasts puff out in the direction of the wisdom-conferring and peace-giving spirals.

She, the uncrowned queen, has not deigned to look upon her lowly, docile subjects. She impassively abandons her relaxed body to the respectful mats, and smokes. In a wink of the eye, the occidental varnish has cracked. There are no more tyrants here to flatter. The soul of the Far-East may now rear itself, sovereignly, above the barbaric mummeries of a conquering race. And the Aeginetic smile which parts the thin opium-blackened lips now resembles, resembles more and more, the smile of those imperial idols which rest forgotten in their crumbling pagodas.

The daughter of Tong-Doc dreams.

She dreams dreams unknown to the Occident;— dreams filled with a philosophy that is too arduous for the intelligence of young races. In the setting of her dream, there hover, undoubtedly, yamens which the Barbarians have not yet polluted, yamens glorying in virgin smoking-rooms, where the dangerous genii of feverish forests are proud to serve, on bended knee, the Princess of the sacred blood. But as for the dream itself, its color, and its outline, and its soul, the gods themselves would not be able to discover anything of all this upon that immobile brow, or in those dark eyes which the Drug has metallized. . . .

Now, however, the Princess stops and lays aside the bamboo pipe. She now casts a look upon the vermin population, curdled with ecstasy amid the black spirals rolling upward from the ground. Is she thinking the Virgin Widow of the Emperors, of a treacherous Destiny, which has robbed her of the obedience of another people, — more numerous, — a human population like to this insect populace, in its immovable respect and in its petrified adoration? Is she weeping, solely, with these sobs of rage, for a dead Empire and a Scepter metamorphosed into a yoke?

Once more, the pipe bends over the lamp, and the silent mouth breathes on the bamboo. The compassionate drug is one that can heal all sorrows. And so, it is with opium that Tong-Doc's daughter sustains her bleeding pride, her tragic pride in a dynasty that is sixty times a hundred years old.

THIRD PERIOD
ECSTASIES

Foochow Road

It has now become my most cherished habit. Each evening, I smoke opium.

Not at home. I do not care to have a layout in my house. I live on the Bund, in the Concession Fran-gaise. Many people come to see me, and that I like, better than you would think: there are always so many absurd stories told about smokers!

No, no one knows it. In the evening, at an hour when Europeans are dozing at the club or carrying on flirtations in the drawing-rooms, I pretend to go home, with a very blase air so far as fashionable life is concerned. And my jinrikisha-man, who is waiting at the door, takes me at once, as fast as his sturdy yellow legs can trot, along the deserted streets which lead to the heart of the Concession Internationale. It is there that I do my smoking, in Foochow Road, Shanghai's merry street.

I have no preferred place. In Foochow, smoking-dens abound, all of them receptive. Shanghai is the city of festivals, the voluptuous rendez-vous of the whole of Yangtze,—a Deauville, Biarritz and Monte Carlo, all in one. And Foochow Road is the Chinese heart of Shanghai. When night comes, the entire street is one red glow of lights. Each door is a den, more or less weird, more or less alluring, but generous in the matter of opium. I enter, at hazard, the first one that strikes my fancy, I stretch out near a lamp that is not in use, and immediately, a boy,—a brat with an old and curdled face,—comes up and prepares the pipe. I never tire of looking at him.

No matter where, he is the same silent, prompt being who never smiles and never bestows a glance. He dips the needle into the little jug filled with sticky opium. Then, over the lamp, he proceeds to cook the pearly drop. The drop swells, grows yellow and buds. He kneads and works it against the bowl of the pipe; he rolls and stretches it, makes it supple,— and finally glues it, with a blunt pressure, to the center of the bowl, against the orifice of the slender stem. As for me, all that I have to do is to suck in, with long-drawn breath, the stale and tepid smoke, while he holds above the flame the black pill, which crackles, diminishes and then evaporates.

The first pipe knocks me out and annihilates me. I lie upon my back, incapable of the batting of an eyelid. And that lasts one, two, three minutes. The patient boy offers me the second pipe, which is ready. But I continue to relish, minutely, the first fruits of my drunkenness; I gluttonously taste the distracted wheelings of my brain, which is not as yet able to undergo phlegmatically the first assault of the divine poison. It is only as the voluptuous vertigo spends itself that I heavily raise my neck and stretch forth my lips for the second pipeful.

There are other smokers around me. I cannot see them clearly, for the reason that the smoking-room is almost in darkness, and for the further reason that we are all reclining, our figures indistinct against the brown mats. But I can see the glow of lights amid the black smoke, and I hear the crackling of numerous pipes, and am conscious of an indescribable odor. I am aware, likewise, that other, neighboring intelligences are sinking simultaneously into drunkenness; and this fills my soul with a fraternal joy and the feeling of an affectionate security. Opium, in reality, is a fatherland, a religion, a strong and jealous tie between men. And I can better feel a brother to the Asiatics smoking in Foochow Road than I can to certain inferior Frenchmen now vegetating at Paris, where I was born.

Formerly, I believed that Asiatics were separated from
my own race by a wide gulf. And in truth, what a bottomless
precipice there is between us! We are children, and they are old
men. There is not so much difference between the infant in arms
and the centenarian, hastening to his grave, as there is between
them and us.

But I know, today, that opium is able, in a marvelous manner,
to scale that precipice. Opium is a magician which transforms,
and works a metamorphosis.

The European, the Asiatic are equal,—reduced to a level,—
in the presence of its all-powerful spell. Races, physiologies,
psychologies,—all are effaced; and other strange new beings are
born into the world, —the Smokers, who, properly speaking,
have ceased to be men.

All this is quite literal. Each evening, in Foochow Road, I
shed my gross humanity, I free myself from it, casting it into
the street like a bundle of rags. I, and all the other smokers like
me. From then on, our renovated brains, the sons of opium and
brothers to one another, at once understand and appreciate each
other, and are friends. Unfortunately, the intoxication is too
brief; and in the morning, as I sorrowfully return to my house
and bed, I abdicate my superiority, and put on those human rags
and tatters once more, while the yellow men of that other race
become for me again closed and indecipherable books.

No matter. Among these same individuals, drunkenness has
given me a few friends.

For a number of evenings, a youth with piercing eyes has
stretched out beside me, in the most gilded of the smoking-dens
in Foochow Road,—a low-ceilinged room, bristling all over with
weird carvings, carefully covered with gilt varnish.—A young
man in a robe of mauve-colored moire, whose lean fingers roll
the opium with a marvelous dexterity. His name is Tcheng-Ta.
His father is a rich merchant. He lives as he likes, in the manner
of an opulent Chinese artist.

Tcheng-Ta has brought me to his own smoking-den, on the mezzanine of one of the most labyrinthine houses in Foochow Road. The entrance is by a perpendicular and very dark alley-way; and then, one has to climb two floors and come down one,—all this being broken by tortuous corridors and narrow court-yards, where one sometimes perceives singular things. . . . And at the very end is Tcheng-Ta's den. It is a very simple whitewashed room, with plenty of mats and cushions on the floor. While one is smoking, Tcheng-Ta's mistress prepares the green tea, or sings, to the accompaniment of a guitar, melodies which resemble very gentle miaulings.

There is no talk between us, for the thoughts we have in common are not such as are easily exchanged in an unfamiliar tongue. But the opium spares us idle words. Our friendly glances are enough. And I know, and he knows, that we are always in a state of perfect communion.

The other day, he surprised the quickly restrained glance which I thoughtlessly had cast upon Ot-Chen, his mistress. Today, he introduced me to Tchen-Hoa, Ot-Chen's sister. They are a pair of dolls, rose-red and white, like painted porcelain. Their amber-perfumed hands are adorably fine, and their bound feet are easily contained within satin slippers the size of two nuts.

Their hair is of curiously wrought ebony, though one catches but a glimpse of it, since they hide it under close-crowded pearls. Tchen-Hoa and Ot-Chen love nothing in the world except jewels. On each arm, they wear sixteen bracelets, and on each finger seven rings. Only for love will they consent to shed their precious sheaths and to present themselves nude, like poor little prostitutes; but once the embrace is over, they hasten to pick up their ornaments before worrying about their scattered clothing.

They smoke opium beside us. Their fingers lay hold of the pipes in a pretty mannered gesture, and their mouths assume subtle pouts before the bamboo which our lips have moistened.

They wear bodices of light-colored moire, trimmed with satin, with very wide sleeves, and above these, other sleeveless bodices. Their pantaloons, which fall straight down to their ankles, are of the same heavy, stiff, sumptuous material, all the seams being concealed under embroideries of the same color as the material itself,—Nile-green, pale mauve or silver-gray.

When the opium has seized me in its clutches and has carried me off in its winged flight, Ot-Chen and Tcheng-Hoa become, in my fancy, two legendary princesses, and I am greatly comforted by dreams which are very ancient and very wonderful. Tcheng-Ta's den becomes a marble palace, sheltering my sovereign indolence, while I know that round about me there exists no longer the tumult of Foochow Road, but the formidable silence of historic forests, where imperial yamens sleep. The pipe-smoke sinks in a fine black dust; and the walls, the mats and the ceiling, where swings an enormous red and yellow lantern, become veiled and shaded with it, become variegated with old and mysterious colors, clothe themselves in bronze, in gold and in ivory, and proudly adorn themselves with giant porcelains and venerable lacquer-work. Favorite Queens offer me Yunnan tea in the imperial goblet, the goblet of green jade. And in a very real fashion, I am the Emperor, Hoang-Ti, the Most Sacred.—But here, memory fails me, and I know no more. What century is this, what dynasty, my dynasty? And why do those unseemly cries pierce my marble walls? Is it that, without remembering, I have transported my capital to those noisy cities which my successors shall prefer,—to Ho-Nam or to Tchin-Tou-Fou? . . .

But no. All is calm, so calm that surely I must have been dreaming but a moment ago. . . . And upon some nameless, invisible seesaw, the opium now rocks me, rocks me to the point of nausea. . . .

The Pipes

In my layout, I have five pipes.

For the reason that China, the source of opium, the source of wisdom, is familiar with five primitive virtues.

* * *

My first pipe is of brown shell, with a black earthenware bowl and two muzzles of light-colored shell.

It is old and precious.

The stem is thick, and opaque or diaphanous according to the marbling of the shell. The knob, which holds the fingers while one is smoking, is an amber-hued projecture, finely carved in the form of a diminutive fox. The bowl is hexagonal, and is fastened in the middle by a silver fang.

In the center of it, the coagulated opium-ash, the dross, bitter and rich in morphine, has been gradually deposited, in the form of thin black pellicles. Therein resides the soul of by-gone pipefuls, the soul of dead intoxications. And the shell, progressively penetrated by the dros, retains among its molecules the vestiges of the years which have flown.

Those are Japanese years. For my first pipe was in Kiou-Siou, the Japanese island of turtles. And in the convex mirror of the wide stem, I can see the whole of Japan reflected.

The fox which forms the knob is not a fox. It is the Kitsoune of legend, the fairy beast which undergoes a metamorphosis at will. And so it is, when I take the shell pipe in my hands, I never fail to examine the knob, to see if it may not, mysteriously, have changed form. If it were to undergo such a change, some fine day, I should not be greatly surprised. The Kitsoune of my pipe must, indeed, be a famous beast, and one wise in sorcery, to have been selected as a model by the artist who did this carving. It is possible that it is the very Kitsoune which, in the old days, misled the heroine Sidzouka in the mountains of Yosino.

The porcelain pipe knows the story of Sidzouka, and sometimes relates it to me in a low tone,—on winter evenings, whilst the opium is budding and crackling above the lamp. Sidzouka was a Japanese lady of noble race, whom the hero Yositsoune loved. Yositsoune lived in Nippon, many centuries ago. A brother of Prince Yoritomo the Terrible, he alone it was who had assured his brother's triumph over the rival clans of Talra. But his enthusiastic samurai had been too loud in proclaiming him the bravest of his race, and the jealous Yoritomo had condemned him to die. The fugitive Yositsoune had wandered for a long time, far from cities, in the solitude of the violet mountains, where only wild-boars climb. Nevertheless, this perilous exile was sweet to him, for the reason that Sidzouka, the sweetest of all, had followed him in his disgrace, and had proudly shared his hardships.

For long, the Japanese forest provided a doubtful shelter for their weariness. The moss-grown cedars mounted careless guard about the proscribed, while the moon, all too white, dangerously silvered the pools of light and the bark of the birch-trees. But at these anxious moments, Sidzouka would dance voluptuously in front of her lover, and the enchanted hero would forget his sorrow, would forget the unrelenting pursuit of the tyrant's soldiery, bent upon hunting him down.

This lasted till the day of grief, when, with the enemy tightening his death-circle, Yositsoune sent his mistress away, preparing to face his destiny alone. Then, before she departed, guided by a faithful samurai, the hero presented his loved one, in token of his tender gratitude, with the tambourine which still serves her as accompaniment in her nocturnal dance, in the wooded solitudes of the mountains of Yosino.

Her eyes blurred with tears, Sidzouka departed. But the samurai, for some mysterious reason, failed to keep faith with her. The path which he had chosen soon plunged into strange and fearful regions, bristling with peaks and riddled with abysses. The terrified lady no longer was able to recognize the way. And as she paused, overcome with fear, the guide, casting off his two sabers and suddenly shedding his human form, became visible, in the last rays of the moon, for what he was,—a long-tailed Kitsoune, bellowing fantastically at the betrayed princess as he danced the Kitsounes' supernatural dance.

With furtive steps, the fairy beast then approached his victim, and Yositsoune's tambourine at once flew to him. For that had been the cause of all the trouble. The Kitsoune had recognized this fox-skin tambourine. A Kitsoune, slain out of revenge, had furnished the parchment for it; and the bewitched instrument logically had returned to its bewitched source. As for Sidzouka, the Ever Faithful, once free of the ill-omened tambourine, she found no difficulty in regaining the right path, and the blue-eyed moon promptly guided her to the convent which she had chosen as the place to weep for her beloved.

.... The shell pipe knows many Japanese stories, and sometimes tells them to me in a low voice, during the winter evenings, while the opium is budding and crackling above the lamp.

* * *

My second pipe is wholly of silver, with a bowl of white porcelain.

It is old and precious.

The extremely long stem is not a thick but a fragile one. This is in order that the pipe may not be too heavy in the smoker's hands. The knot is a massive silver projecture, carved in the form of a rat. And the bowl, carefully polished, is as round as a little snowball.

The whole length of the pipe has been engraved by the
artist with marvelous Chinese ornaments. For my second pipe
is Chinese,—Cantonese. It speaks to me of that south of China,
where I once passed some very charming years.

Coiled about the silver pipe are flowers, leaves and grasses.
The flowers are the beautiful hibiscus in bloom; the leaves are
leaves of wild mint; and the grasses are rice-stalks. All this
exhales a delicious odor of the China of Kwang-tung, with its
cool lanes, its fertile rice-fields and its pretty villages'squatting in
groves of trees.

Coiled about the silver pipe are men and women. The
men are, alternately, laborers and pirates; and both groups are
courteous and impassive. The women are the daughters of Pak-
Hoi, of Now-Chow or of Hainan. Their soft skin gleams like
amber-colored satin. Their hands and feet would make the most
noble of our marquises jealous. Ot-Che, my mistress, where are
you? It is your memory that haunts me now, the memory of your
fingers so expert in handling the needle, as I dream on amid the
black smoke, the silver pipe resting in my hands.

My third pipe is of ivory, with a white-jade bowl and two
muzzles of green jade.

It is older and more precious than the first two.

It is carved in the form of an elephant's tusk. It is very thick,
and so heavy that one guesses it to have been made for the men
of old, who were more robust than we. The knot is of bark, and
is in the form of a rustically carved ape. The square bowl gleams
like milk which has been turned green by the adding of a little
pistachio, while opaque serpentine veins twine about the middle
of the transparent jade.

The ivory pipe was formerly white, white as the western
race, which conquers the elephants beyond the mountains. But
the patient dros has yellowed and then browned it, little by little,
until it is today like the opium-smoking oriental race. Thus, the
souls of the two rival races mingle—in the ivory pipe.

Fertile India, swarming from the Ganges to the Deccan; wise Thibet, crouched upon her snowy steppes; nomadic Mongolia, where the gawky camels trot; China, countless and divine, China, imperial and philosophic:—the ivory pipe mysteriously evokes the whole of Asia.

For it is old, older than many civilizations. I happen to know that an Occidental Queen,—Persian, Tartar, Scythian?—presented it, one historic day, to the Chinese Emperor who had come to visit her, all of thirty centuries ago. I used to know the name of the Queen and the name of the Emperor, but the disdainful opium has swept them from my memory, and all that I can remember is the noble and peace-inspiring tale of those great rulers who came, one hastening to anticipate the other, across the breadth of their empires, to exchange, across frontiers which were no more, vows of concord which were like to vows of love. Thirty times a hundred years.... . Ivory pipe, how many imperial mouths have pressed you to them since that time? How many Majesties, clad in yellow silk, have sought in your cradling kiss forget-fulness of their sorrows and of their cares, forgetful-ness of the ruin and injuries which, growing each day more bitter, were falling upon the Sacred Empire of the Hoang-Ti's. And if I behold you now tarnished and blackened, is that merely the mourning which you wear, mourning for all the wise centuries that have died to make way for this century of ours, so light and frivolous?

* * *

I do not know of what it is my fourth pipe is made. It is my father's pipe, and he died from smoking it.

It is a murderous pipe. It is saturated with dross saturated in all its pores and in all its fibers. Ten poisons, all of them ferocious ones, lie ambushed in its black cylinder, which is like the trunk of a venomous cobra.—Morphine, codeine, narcotine,— what others? My father died from having smoked too much, and the opium, evaporating in this pipe-bowl of his, takes on the mysterious odor of death.

It is a funereal pipe. "Wholly black, on account of the dross, and plated with gold-chasings, which shine like coffin-trappings. I dare not bring it near my mouth,—not as yet. But often, I gaze upon it,—as one gazes upon a tomb which stands ajar,—with desire and with dizziness.

My father died from having smoked it,—my father whom I loved. Between life and death,—life ugly and futile, death serene and prolific in marvelous intoxications,—he chose death. When the day shall have come, I shall do as he did.

And I shall seek, upon the black gold-plated pipe, the cold taste of paternal lips,—seek it devoutly.

* * *

And now, the lamp is lighted, the mats are on the floor, and the green tea is steaming in the cups without handles.

And here is my fifth pipe, all ready for me. It is not old, and it is not precious. I purchased it of the coffin-maker for six taels. It is a plain brown bamboo, finished off with a red-earth bowl. The bamboo knob is sufficient to give a grip to the fingers.

It has no gold nor jade nor ivory. No prince, no queen has smoked it. It does not evoke, in magic fashion, poetically distant provinces nor centuries of past glory.

But all the same, it is the one which I prefer above all the others. For it is this one that I smoke,—not the others; they are too sacred.—It is this one which, each evening, pours an intoxicating draft for me, opening for me the dazzling door to clear-headed pleasures, bearing me triumphantly away, out of life and to those subtle spheres which opium-smokers know: those philosophic and beneficent spheres where dwell Hwang-Ti, the Sun-Emperor; Kwong-Tsu, the Perfectly Wise; and the God without a Name who was the first of smokers.

The Tigers

My smoking-room is not upholstered with mats. I despise the rattan from Hong-Kong and the bamboo from Foochow. On the walls, I have not cared to have any unrolled kakemonos, with horned gods grinning from pagoda-studded landscapes.

From top to bottom, from head to foot,—from the floor where the wan lamp keeps watch to the cornices where slumber the highest-soaring whiffs,— my den is tapestried with tiger-skins, with rude yellow skins, striped with black, quartering in all directions a sharp thicket of heavy claws.

Heads, revived by means of green-enamel eyes, hang from the walls or flatten out upon the floor. By this arrangement, the ones provide pillows for the smokers' necks, while the others, ranged in a circle, keep watch over the intoxications of the dreamers. Surrounded by this ferocious coterie, I enjoy a greater peace and more repose.

Formerly, in that part of China where I first became acquainted with the mellow quality of pipes, I believed I had to aid the kindly drug with a bizarre and sumptuous setting. I picked out those dives in Canton where the knives of stranger-haters, more than once, came near molting my drunkenness into death. I picked out those yamens in Pekin, where the women, dressed as idols, mingled soothing songs and voluptuous dances with the charms of opium. I picked out those polished, courteous places frequented by the rarest spirits, loving to season my enjoyment with the subtle salt of philosophic discussions. I even chose, upon occasion, those lewd resorts where opium is but a veil for disguised lubricities and vicious platitudes, rebelliously

seeking to erect themselves into—satanism.—But today, opium
has washed me clean of my curiosity-seeking restlessness; and I
have no longer any need of intricate frame, lascivious woman or
eloquent philosopher. I smoke alone, in the midst of my striped
body-guard, with their gleaming teeth; and I would do the same
in an empty room, with walls devoid of covering. However, I
prefer my tigers, for the reason that their fur keeps out the cold of
pallid mornings, and because I love, in my drunkenness, to rest
my eyes upon the black and yellow geometry with which they
zebra-stripe my walls. I no longer dream, as I look upon them, of
those barbaric forests over which they once played the tyrant. I
no longer dream of red evenings rudely swooping down upon the
jungles, of sudden sunsets timidly lighting the striped hunter's
awakening, or of his deep yawn and the famished stretching
of his claws. I no **longer dream of his sharp baying, which**
once was heard in the Tonkin night, of that baying which throws
the cattle in the stables into an uproar. No, my tigers no longer
call up for me the phantasmagoria of old and distant visions. I
have been a smoker for too long a time. The world of men and
of things, the world of life itself, is too far removed from me.
There is nothing in common between that world and my present
thought. My tigers please me merely because their skins are soft,
and supply me with a diverting bizarrerie.

I no longer worry about anything; I no longer have any trade,
any friends;—I smoke. Opium, each day, plunges me deeper
within myself. And I find it sufficiently interesting to enable me
to forget all that is outside.

There was a time when I permitted myself to be seduced
chiefly by the *sorcery* of opium. It appeared to me to be a
wonderful thing to have a part in those metamorphoses which
the drug works among its faithful followers. It appeared to me to
be a sublime thing to offer my body to its transforming power of
fantasy. I relished the ravishing sensation of becoming a different
animal, with senses atrophied or multiplied,—the ravishment of
no longer seeing and of hearing better, of no longer tasting and

of feeling more deeply; and I relished, also, the exasperation of my tactile nerves and the torpor of my sexual organs. But these trifles have ceased to attract me, since the opium has penetrated my brain sufficiently to make possible, at last, a revelation of the true wisdom.

What is more, the mere physical pleasure of the pipes,—one, however, which my body finds indispensable,—the pleasure of smoking, in itself, now constitutes but a small fraction of the delight I encounter in the act. Certainly, no spasm of the heart or marrow is comparable to the radiant rape of the lungs by that black smoke. And I am today more skillful than ever before, as I pantingly meet the gentle, treacherous kiss of the drug; I am skillful in becoming tipsy with its warm odor, skillful in cleverly enjoying, to the utmost, the multiple itching which riddles my arms and my belly with subtle prickings; and I am skillful, too, in the anxious watch I keep for that fatal torpor which, each day, is squeezing my neck more tightly, and which, little by little, is slowly but surely destroying my muscles and my bodily members.— And yet, all this unspeakable felicity of flesh is as nothing beside my ecstatic joy of thought.

Oh, to feel one's self becoming, from second to second, less carnal, less human, less earthly; to lie in watch for the free flight of mind escaping from matter, the soul unfettered from the lobes of the brain; to marvel at the mysterious multiplication of noble faculties,—intelligence, memory, sense of the beautiful; to become, in the course of a few pipe-fuls, the veritable equal of heroes, of apostles and of gods; to understand, without an effort, the thought of a Newton, to command the genius of a Napoleon, to correct the faults in taste of a Praxitiles; to bring together, finally, within one heart, which has become too vast, all virtues, all goodness, all tenderness; to love beyond measure the whole of heaven and the whole of earth, to blend in one gentle fragrance enemies and friends, good and bad, happy and miserable:— surely, the Olympus of the Greeks and the Paradise of Christians have no blessedness so overflowing in store for their elect. And yet, such are my blessings!

In truth, the religions that I used to despise from the peaks of a philosophy which I now perceive to have been a trifle empty,— the philosophy of the Nietzsches of the earth,—those same religions are by no means wrong in exalting charity and mercy above justice and pride. For my joy in surpassing all men in my genius yields, strangely enough now, to my joy in being the best, the least in need of pity, among men. Out of this superiority of my own heart over all other hearts is born a warmly felt and inexpressible satisfaction. Generous souls, tormented with the ideal and the beyond, frequently know the bitter pain of life, for the reason that life appears to them vile and ugly, blackened with evil. But as for me, I see more clearly, and I have ceased to see the evil. From the fifteenth pipe on, evil is effaced from my sight. At a single glance, I then take in each effect in all its causes, each gesture in all its motions, each crime in all its excuses. And the causes and the excuses, their name is legion, so that, all too equitable and all too clear-headed a judge that I am, I never can bring myself either to condemn or to curse,— but only to absolve, to commiserate and to love. And over my smoke-sprinkled skins, Cain, Judas or Brutus would meet with the same reception as would Caesar or Kwong-Tsu.

And now that I reflect upon it, that is why I have strewn my den with tiger skins. These tigers, ferocious, treacherous, sacrilegious, are my Cains, my Judases and my Brutuses. Their snouts, ill-cleansed of blood, their skulls flattened out over rudimentary brains, and the perfidious suppleness of their spines, over which I run my fingers,—everything about them speaks to me of the deplorable imperfection of this world, a world that is, yet, all too excusable, even in its worst mistakes, for me ever to dare condemn it.

And I have no ill feelings whatsoever against my tigers for having, in their jungles of old, defiled with blood those blue light-pools where the moon stooped to meet Endymion's lips.

Interlude

The door closed upon the last trouble-maker, shutting out the hostile darkness of the corridor; and in the den, there was none left but the true initiates. Upon the ceiling, shadows danced, only to melt in a gilded chiaroscuro. None too diaphanous spirals rolled heavily upward from the lamp, and the despotic odor of opium alone reigned, all rival perfumes having been annihilated: the perfume of Turkish cigarettes, smoked during intermissions; the perfume from the flask of *jicky,* poured drop by drop over hands blackened by the drug; even the perfume, at once gentler and more tenacious, from the half-nude woman smoker, whose body, steeped in kisses, became a glowing incense-pan. Fraternal bodies mingled and huddled more closely together upon the mats; and in the gentle intoxication of the moment, the hours glided by with footfalls so smooth that one no longer heard them.

Itala, whose neck rested upon the woman-smoker's groin, was the first to break the silence.

"I have loved you much," he said, "and I still love you, with anguished desire, despite the fact that you have given yourself to your new lover. But I hold nothing against you for that, even at this moment, which you have chosen as the one in which to caress him. For the kindly drug enables me, when I so wish it, to relive the days gone-by, when your body was mine and mine alone;—and to live also, the days to come, when, tired and sick at heart, you shall return to my cradling arms. And so it is, I forget your happy sighs of the present, in delightedly sharing your sighs of yesterday and of tomorrow. But as I say, I hold nothing against you, thanks to opium."

Without ceasing to tighten her thighs about the head of the lover whom she loved, the woman-smoker complacently turned aside her lips from the waiting pipe and extended them to Itala.

The other, Timour, whose Tartar profile was barely distinguishable against the brown-silk cushion, likewise spoke out frankly, although he was always a prudent and a secretive man:

"Women, in truth, though each one asserts that she is 'not like the others,' are marvelously all alike. When I was Laurence de Trailles' lover, she did not love me, and I did not love her. I merely had turned her bird-like head, by reading her thoughts too correctly, and she came straight to my arms, just as she would have run to a sleep-walker. She was incapable of any emotion other than the false and childish sentimentality of young girls reared in a convent. She sensed my indifference, without suffering from it.

" 'Your love for me is a game, isn't it?'

"She laughed, finding that the game affected her nerves, which were eager to be stirred. But just the same, in spite of her emotional drought, her perverse-ness and the relished taste of new kisses, she never absolutely abandoned conjugal love. Her husband, the beast, was madly in love and jealous. By no means a complex individual, he was always, in her eyes, an eventual refuge, the port where one ended by going ashore, after putting into a number of other sensual harbors. And even on our most sportive days, I can remember that she never forgot to give her lips, complacently, to her spouse; just as our friend here has offered you hers,—offered them to you, her intermittent lover, that is to say, a sort of husband."

The third, Aneyr, the lover who was loved, would have spoken; but his mistress, tired of opium, clasped his body and clung to his lips, so long that he was able to say nothing.

Then, Itala asked a question.

"You deceived Trailles, then, who was your friend. And yet, you were not in love with his wife. Do you feel any regrets?"

"No. His stupidity in attaching any value whatsoever to sexual fidelity rendered him deserving of punishment for his sin. What is more, his boorish-ness, in conjunction with Laurence's empty frivolity, could never have produced any children that would not have been perfect dunces. Whereas, my own nomadic conqueror's blood, which I have mingled, in voluptuous drops, with the blood of their veins, will beget, it may be, a son of my own better and loftier race."

Aneyr, releasing his mouth from the hungry one which clung to it, said:

"The pleasure which you found in your embraces is sufficient to absolve you, without need of anything else. The prophet has stated the thing with perspicacity: Each cry of joy from your wives opens wider for you the gates of Paradise."

"That," said Timour, "is a Mohammedan postulate, which I cannot admit, for ethnographic reasons. First of all, I have little faith in Paradise. And I in no wise feel the need of legitimatizing my perfectly legitimate act. Hypocritical old maids and castrated Huguenots are the only persons in the world who would censure the natural embrace of two properly suited beings, under the comic pretext that the lover happens to have a wife or the mistress a husband. A tremendously philosophic argument, that! It is admitted that a woman may freely dispose of her hand or her cheek, extending them *to* such friendly lips as she may see fit. Yet, similar caresses with mouth or vagina are forbidden. To tell the truth, I might have found grace even with those most hardened by prejudice, since in loving Laurence, I was thinking very often of finer children than any she would, otherwise, have been able to conceive."

"And that," murmured Aneyr, "is what one might **term** the justification of cuckoldom through anxiety over proper paternity."

They fell silent. Itala smoked pipe after pipe. Aneyr, his body half freed from that of his sweetheart, plied the needle. For moments at a time, the smoker, letting the bamboo go, would throw his enraptured head back upon the cushions. The silent smoking-den became immobile. No agitation was apparent upon the clear, pensive, faces, and there was no longer any motion to deform the clarity of line.

"A layout," observed Timour, "is as beautiful a thing as a fragment of ancient Greece."

In her turn, the woman brought the bamboo to her mouth. Then, having breathed on the pipe, she stretched herself out like a cat and began walking on her hands and knees. Her unclasped Japanese robe trailed over the reclining bodies. In that medley of legs and arms, it was not easy to find a place. But feminine nerves are amorously played upon by opium, and the woman who thus brushed the other smokers was not seeking a mat as a resting-place. She hesitated. The three male bodies exhibited an equal degree of suppleness and strength in repose. Timour, whose eyes were closed, all at once felt the warm embrace of two arms, slipping under his shoulder, and the caress of a mouth sucking violently at his tongue. He abandoned himself from the start, without emotion,—for opium appeases and **overpowers virility**,—without emotion, for the reason that he was thinking of Laurence de Trailles and of similar sensualities on her part,— thinking of this and of countless other things. Aneyr had risen, indifferently, to seek amusement in a cigarette. Itala was smoking.

How much time elapsed? Hours or minutes? Timour's drowsy senses slowly awake, and he returns cafess for caress, as he dreams aloud his thought.

"Aneyr, go to sleep. I want her. Don't look."

And Aneyr's voice, heavy with black smoke:

"Wait till I finish my cigarette."

But suddenly, the amorous one frees herself from the embrace, having been recalled by the voice of her loved one to her real preference. And it is against Aneyr's flesh that she now passionately hurls her animated body. They entwine as they stand erect, she greedily, he in a surprised and impotent manner. Close at hand, the divan offers its favoring back.

Timour, obliviously, has taken his place beside the lamp, opposite Itala. They smoke in turn, no longer conscious of anything that goes on about them. The groaning of the hard-pressed divan has no effect on them, any more than has the enervated sigh of the woman whom her lover cannot satisfy.

Itala murmurs:

"Timour, you are the most perfect of us all. Tell me how it was your mother set about it to give birth to a son like you, and how it was your father made love to her nine months before, on that milky night which he selected to beget you."

Timour murmurs:

"They have forgotten. And those, indeed, are secrets of which men and the gods are ignorant. That kiss from which Hercules was born, Alcmene and Zesu themselves never have been able to give again."

A lament, a sob of exasperated desire, then a trampling of nude feet over the mats. The woman has snatched herself from her lover's embrace and runs away a few steps, only to come back at once, a flask in her hand. But the smokers behold only the heavy spirals which clothe the room in mystery. Upon the noisy divan, the lovers' struggle begins anew. But the smokers hear only the crackling of the opium above the lamp. More satisfying caresses now, and the two bodies in the act of love exhale a more provoking perfume. But the smokers scent only the odor of the drug, sovereign.. ..

And now, suddenly, the pipe slips from Itala's hands, and Timour straightens up, his nails dug into the earth. Above the opium-tray, their sobered eyes meet.

"You smell it?"

"Yes."

The black smoke eddies, as though distracted.

A terrifying thing happens. In the opium-saturated den, filled with odorous atoms, peaceful and triumphant, other atoms now burst tumultuously: an invasion of terror and of death. A dull pallid smell attacks the friendly odor of opium and subjugates it. Conflicting effluvia violently collide in the subject air, and the potent opium is thinned out, effaced, decomposed, vanquished.

Ether. . . .

Glacial ether, cousin to madness and to hypnosis...

The dangerous flask has been overturned upon the divan. It is thus that the woman, in her most unsati-ated hours, seeks solace for her painful libido. Quick, demented cries gush forth:

"Never, never more. . . . Not him, Oh, no, not him! I won't have it! Too late, too late. . . ."

The opium-smokers are on their feet, fiercely shuddering.

Itala speaks.

"Was I telling you that I loved her. I lied! I don't love her any more."

And Timour:

"Laurence. ... I didn't speak your name, did I? I didn't speak it? It's not true, it's not true. ... ."

FOURTH PERIOD
DOUBTS

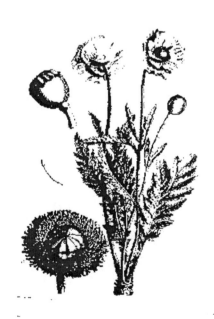

Rodolph Hafner's Two Souls

To Henri de Regnier

D ID RODOLPH HAFNER, as a matter of fact, have two souls? That is what I believed, but I am aware that the supposition is a very odd one. All sorts of respectable institutions, such as religion and philosophy, appear to establish the point, to the contrary, that he could have had but one,—or else none at all, in accordance with the accepted doctrine,—one soul, or no soul. But two, that is ridiculous and insane.

All the same, I believe, for my part, that Rodolph Hafner had two souls, which inhabited his body one after the other. To tell the truth, the first one may not really have been his. It may have been a sort of wandering soul, momentarily substituted, through some farcical trick on the part of the powers of darkness, for Hafner's own soul, which was the second of the two. If that is how things were, that wandering soul is, undoubtedly, still wandering through the world, in quest of a new body to give it lodging. In which case, I should love to meet up with it, even at the risk of losing my own soul (through a new sub*stitution), for I was peculiarly in love with that first soul of Rodolph* **Hafner's.**

It was with that soul that I came to know him. Come to think of it, where did I meet him first? I am no longer quite sure. We girdled the globe for so long together. Moreover, my memory has become something dreadful, since I took to smoking Indian

opium in place of Chinese.—No matter, I'll recall it in a moment.
What I am certain of is that it was in a Creole country. You do
not know what Creoles are. Soft and languorous beings, who live
in hammocks, swinging under the palms? No, not that. I shall not
explain to you what they are, for that would bore me too much.

Ah, now that I recall, it was at New Orleans that I saw
Rodolph Hafner for the first time,—a very vibrant city. I had
been there eight days, having come because I had nothing better
to do. One evening, in the drawing room of the Rouths (very fine
people in St. Charles Avenue), the daughter of the house, who
was a chum of mine, promised me for the following day a quite
unusual pleasure-party. She had tickets for a "regulation ring"
(for these folk simply murdered the English language). The affair
in hand was an unusual bout between two young women, two
women of the better class, moreover, who had decided to settle a
little difference between them with their fists, in the presence of a
circle of male and female friends.

These Creole matinees on the part of the Yankee ladies
are quite astonishing. The latter can do nothing behind closed
doors, not even frizzle their hair. My chum supplied me with the
details in the present instance. This was not a case of a simple, if
rather far-fetched, sporting challenge. No, a real battle was to be
fought,—for keeps, so to speak. There had been hatred, jealousy,
treachery, goodness knows what; and a regulation challenge had
followed. There was sure, therefore, to be a merciless struggle,
quite exciting, and probably ferocious. Naturally, I went.

It was, indeed, ferocious and as exciting as one could wish.
The two combatants were as like one another as two drops of
water,—the same figure, the same ebony hair, even the same
warm and striking complexion, the same vigorous and supple
bodies, the same profiles—the profiles of a pair of pretty, sensual
beasts. That is the prevailing type of Louisiana Creole, and I can
assure you, it is a very seductive one. They went for each other
furiously, after the English fashion, their hands provided with

big boxing-gloves, their heads and throats bare. They wore, by way of undress costume, identical comic opera effects: black-silk tights; trusses of puffed satin; and little light-colored bodices, trimmed with invisible bits of lace. In a quarter of an hour, their costumes were in tatters. They hit home for all that was in them, furious at the mutual disfiguration they were inflicting. Two French women would have made an end of it, in the wink of an eye, by throwing a fit of hysteria. But these two belabored each other, patiently, for sixty-five minutes by the clock,—six rounds with no result, the seventh fought to a finish.

There is no need to say that from the second round, the spectacle was more repulsive than a dog-fight. With bloody, piteously swollen faces, mangled breasts and shoulders covered with black and blue stripes, the two women continued to hammer each other with all their might, with no cries, no tears, like the dumb brutes they were. And as I turned away, sickened, I saw, a little to one side,—looking on, it is true, but without that ferocious gleam which was to be observed in all the other eyes, creole or Yankee,— a slender, fine-featured, beardless man, whose forehead bulged white as ivory under his superbly somber hair, and whose splendid eyes, a sapphire-blue, had the metallic reflection of a pair of steel blades.

I was very impulsive in those days, with nothing to inhibit my first impulses. Rodolph Hafner conquered me upon the instant, to such an extent that I walked directly over to him and took his hand.

"How does it come," I said, "that *you* are watching this disgusting spectacle?"

He looked me over for a few moments, with no surprise. Then, as his glance went back to the ring:

"It is a civilized pleasure," he remarked, "to come upon a primitive instinct in the nude."

And he squeezed my hand.

The moment before, my chum, the little Routh girl, who had been devouring the duelling pair with her eyes, had interlaced her fingers, nervously, with my own. It was at the moment of a tragic clutch, and in that pressure of a child's fingers, I had sensed all that there was of a sadistic sensuality, provoked by the brutal sight in front of us. Hafner squeezed my hand more firmly yet; but in his clasp, there was neither sensuality nor emotion. He was absolutely calm, the master of his nerves. Our hands were clasped out of sympathy solely, a sudden and mutual sympathy. There was between us, from that instant, an extraordinarily intimate friendship, which lasted for very long, up to the time of our separation.

"What a weird thing," he went on, after a moment, and this time without taking his eyes off the fight. "All this, when summed up, is merely a corollary to Newton's laws."

I am sure that if any other person had addressed this elliptic phrase to me, I should have smiled uncomprehendingly. But no sooner had Hafner uttered it than it became instantaneously clear in my brain, as though he had communicated to me, through an occult spell, his own mental deductions, from beginning to end. I knew, without any doubt about the matter, that it was jealousy which had brought these two disfigured women together in the arena, and that, jealousy being but a corollary of love, one might, without paradox, correlate with the attraction of the sexes,—as a little-understood manifestation of that universal attraction,—all that was taking place before our eyes. The syllogism appeared to me to be an obvious one,—indeed, irrefutable; and accordingly, I replied, very sincerely:

"Why weird? It is perfectly natural." Our hands had not yet parted. Once more, I felt his grip, a familiar one this time. And my heartsick-ness was strangely diverted by this contact. A part of his calm entered into me. A mysterious exchange of cerebral effluvia took place between us. I now looked on as he

did, dispassionately and with curiosity. There was a lull. The
two panting rivals were given a chance to get their wind, and
were sponged and rubbed down like race-horses. It seemed that
their eyes were gazing in our direction; but this was merely
an impression. Immediately, they were facing each other once
more. This was the finish-round, and God knows that a fight to
the finish is a particularly hideous thing; it is no longer a fight,
but an execution. The one who is to be vanquished is spotted at
once, and it is simply a question of beating down her resistance,
of giving her all she can stand in the way of punishment. Bur
in spite of all this, I looked on without any effort, the same as
Hafner. I saw one of the rivals, stupefied and blinded, stagger
twice under the blows which rained upon her face. I saw her
fists give up the struggle, as her elbows, raised in front of her
forehead, attempted one last instinctive defense, the touching
gesture of **a** little girl, endeavoring to shun too hard a slap;
and lastly, I saw her swooning body bend and sink under the
knockout blow, which wrenched from her the groan of a lacer-
ated beast. It was the end. They led out the victor, who had
received scarcely less in the way of punishment; and it was my
duty to take once more the arm of the shuddering Miss Routh.

But Hafner did not leave me. He desired to be presented to
the young lady.

And then only did I become conscious of the **fact** that I
knew nothing at all about him, not even his name. He smiled
at my embarrassment and introduced himself: Rodolph Hafner,
stranger. That was all he said; but for that matter, I have always
thought it a comical custom for men to feel called upon to give
you detailed information concerning the trade that enslaves them,
and the bed in which, once upon a time, their father turned their
mother over on her back. As if there were anything in all that of
which to boast.

We ate crayfish together, at Mers—you know the place?
The brewhouse in the English quarter. And I there heard my
friend talk for the first time. His conversation was indescribably

charming. Neither the verbal fireworks of wits nor the well-
fed and beefy phrase of the deep-thinkers. No, but there was a
grace to it, a lightness, a dream-like poetry, along with, here and
there, quite by chance as the idea led up to it, a disconcerting
paradox, a new and sublime truth, or an unlooked for but taken-
for-granted crudity; and in each corner of his thought, there was
an element of the unknown, of the indecipherable, of the beyond.
The conversation of a phantom, turned poet, philosopher and
human being. However, I never should be able to give you an
exact impression of it, and all that I have written about it bears
no more likeness to the subject than a she-ape's grin does to La
Gioconda's smile.

He left us almost immediately. I say "almost immediately,"
for the reason that it seemed that way to me. In reality, we
remained together until evening.

He left us to go smoke, he said, for a half-hour before
dressing for dinner. He was dining out.

"Where," I indiscreetly inquired, and without even stopping
to think that this was none of my business.

"At Madame B.'s," he replied, without any hesitation, "the
one who took part in the fight just now"; and he went away, after
having made an appointment with me for that evening.

No sooner had he left than I became aware that Miss Routh
was madly in love with him. It was the first time she had seen
him, and she was a virtuous girl. And yet, three days later, she
became his mistress,—almost forced herself upon him, for he did
not want her.

The seductive power of this man was really enormous. From
that first evening, I was aware that it was over him the two
women in the "regulation ring" had fought. He took me into his
confidence in the matter, without any fatuous show of mystery.
Not that this was any indiscretion on his part, for we were
already as one soul in two bodies. That first evening, he took me
home with him to his smoking-den, a sanctuary which he never

opened to any one. Contrary to the taste of all the smokers whom I knew, he only cared to smoke alone. From then on, we smoked together, but this, in reality, introduced no change whatsoever. Our processes of thought were so mutually gauged that we had no need to speak in order to carry on a conversation. And the silence of the smoking-room remained, thus, undisturbed by our incessant interchange of unuttered words.

Each of us knew all about the other. And when I say all, I mean, all that the other thought and felt. As for my friend's outward life, his relations, his antecedents, the amount of his fortune, his nationality, I never concerned myself with those things. Even his physical appearance was never extremely familiar to me. Today, as I seek to recall his profile, I am conscious that the one which lives again for me is the profile of the later Hafner, of that other one, not of the one who was formerly my friend, and with whom I lived on terms of absolute intimacy. Now, as for this second Hafner,—the one in whom the second soul found lodging,—I saw him twice, in all, as I am about to explain to you.

But as for the first one, it is in the marrow of my bones, rather than upon my eyeballs, that he has left an ineffaceable imprint. For almost three whole years, we did not stir a foot from each other's side. Through what ominous combination of fortuitous circumstances this came about, I am no longer able to inform you. His career—and by the way, I have not told you that he was something or other in one of the embassies, since it was purely by accident that I myself came to know it—his fantastic career had taken him into the five corners of the globe. I myself have no profession and no fatherland. And so, it came about that there was not a clime, not a continent, not a sea which we did not come to know together, and which I do not still associate with his memory. And if it is true that his soul, that first soul of his, now haunts the places which he once frequented, it is, then, throughout the entire world that I must go look for him.

Everywhere, the *fumerie* followed us, the same *fumerie* we
had used that first evening. You may well believe that I have
seen many such in my time, but I never have seen any the like of
this. The ordinary *fumeries* are half-barren rooms, upholstered
with mats which are more or less Chinese, and adorned with
lanterns, with screens and with parasols, being large enough to
accommodate, at the least, four or five persons. But this one of
ours rather resembled a coffin, being barely big enough for our
two bodies, as they lay in it side by side. It was of arched wicker-
work, with a lining, and was carried folded up in a small case. No
mats; merely an Aubusson rug. No Chinese trinkets, nothing but
the stitched silk, which rounded up into a low vaulted roof and
fell down in walls around the smokers.—It was Hafner's creed
that opium is not a Chinese, but a universal habit.—This stitched
silk quickly became impregnated with the black smoke. The
spirals, imprisoned in the narrow space, saturated it with so intoxicating an odor that, after a few pipefuls, there was no longer
any need for us to smoke: all we had to do was to breathe in the
opium which remained, and the divinest of dreams thus came to
us without any further effort on our part.

It was not, however, the same dream for the two of us. ... .

The opium acted strangely upon Hafner. His reactions
did not tally with any of the usual ones. And yet, those usual
reactions are multiform,—I call upon all smokers to bear me
witness,—and it is weirdly audacious to speak of anything new
in connection with opium. But the truth is, Rodolph Hafner, even
in this, was not like other men.

The drug did not confer upon him the gift of drunkenness,
that normal intoxication which rivets one down, deliciously but
irresistibly, to the earth, while leaving one, at the same time,
lighter, more supple and more subtle than a disembodied spirit.
If Rodolph Hafner sometimes remained for whole hours in that
coffin of a smoking-den, it was simply that he might follow, in
the undulating caprices of the black smoke, the energetic flight

of his thoughts. And he was able, whenever he pleased, to rise, without suffering and without nausea, to clothe himself and to go immediately about his business.

As a logical consequence, opium refused him the gift of exteriorization, that marvelous gift which enables the smoker, for a time, to escape from life, from his age and from himself, and to be no longer an individual but an unlimited particle of matter, foreign to all bodies, and the contemporary in his own fantasy either of Cleopatra or of the thirtieth century. Hafner was always Hafner. He did not become, even, a Hafner less inhibited, or one who was an abler thinker. As he was in his smoking-den, so he was everywhere. The opium remained in him, in a latent state. Less energetic, less overwhelming, less lasting. I have seen Hafner deprive himself of opium for twelve whole hours,— twelve hours! I never could have done that, not even in those days.

I remember the occasion; it was at a ball. We had not smoked since dinner. He danced till dawn, scintillating and indefatigable. Then, he wanted to gamble. I left him to go back to the pipes. When I returned, it was broad daylight. He was still playing. Opium had made him a good gambler, and he had won an impressive sum, never ceasing, all the time, to converse and smile as though it were barely midnight. But then,—and this is deeply engraved in my memory; not even Indian opium shall ever efface it,— then it was I witnessed an alarming sight,— alarming even for me, a smoker.

Hafner, all of a sudden, dropped his cards and did not speak. A tragic anguish was depicted upon his face, and I can swear to you that I saw his soul fluttering in his eyes, ready to take flight. Any one else would have assumed that he was ill; but I understood: the oil was burning low in the lamp, and the flame was dying down. There was barely time. I took him by the arm and led him away quickly for a smoke. All the glow had already been extinguished in his wan eyes.—I have thought since that his body was like a constant-current storage-battery, a storage-battery for opium, where energy is accumulated. So long as there is a particle of this energy left, the engine appears to be fully charged and runs at a uniform speed. But when the last atom has been consumed, it stops abruptly. Hafner had stopped that morning.

Yes, he was exactly that: a storage-battery for opium. That divinity which the kindly drug distributes among its followers,—some squander it, prodigally, in a few seconds, and are then genuinely gods; but Hafner conserved it over a period of hours, and was endowed thus, for hours at a time, with a human sublimity,—that even and sustained sublimity which was his daily life.

Acting as others dream, under the stimulating lash of opium, he was a man of deeds as well as a thinker. This junction is, ordinarily, achieved only by Far-Eastern souls, which are older and more highly civilized than our Aryan ones. But Rodolph Hafner's soul,—his first soul, the one fed on opium,—was not an Aryan soul. Adepts in the occult will tell you that humanity undergoes a series of successive evolutions. In the course of each evolution, new men replace their predecessors, and civilization takes a step forward. We have reached, according to their calculations, the fourth stage; but occasionally, nature makes a mistake and mixes in with our group an individual of the stage to come; and then, we have genii, magi and prophets, beings who appear to belong to no age and to no race. Rodolph Hafner's soul was on visiting-terms with the greatest of these.

He was a man of action. His exceedingly refined and delicate being, capable of all the shadings, and capable of experiencing all the penumbras of existence, would become, frequently, audacious and prompt to act, when confronted by the material difficulties of life. Almost a professional lover, the simultaneous possessor of many women always, Hafner found his way out of the midst of intrigues with the bold and easy bearing of one of

Dumas' musketeers. Today, those adventures of his impress me but little. In my conception, widened under the serene influence of opium, woman is no longer more than a garment of the soul, differing little from the garments of men, while the difference between the sexes is barely a pretext for more or less agreeable contacts, but contacts which are in nowise deserving of their exaggerated reputation. In days gone by, I should have thought differently about the matter, as all of us do when we are a trifle too young. And upon occasion, for hours at a time, I would prove a traitor to opium for the pleasure, or even the possibility, of possessing women. Hafner did the same; and I was, more than once, astonished at the cold-blooded resolution which he then displayed.

That is one fact which has stayed with me, among a hundred which have slipped through the crannies of my brain. I do not know just where it happened, but it was somewhere in France. Hafner was paying a visit to a lady of the world. In the empty drawingroom, conversation languished; gestures followed words, and the sofa was conveniently near at hand—the lady, all of a sudden, yielded. In the midst of their embrace, the hostile maid, who was devoted to the husband's interests, happened in. A stupid situation, but one solved in the wink of an eye. Night was coming on, a rainy winter night. The provincial street outside was deserted. Hafner seized the girl, bound and gagged her, carried her off to his coupe, and took her home and locked her up in his own house,—which, being the consulate, was inviolable territory.—He kept her there for three months, a prisoner in a cellar. She died. He buried her there. Some would call that a crime. It seemed to me then that it was merely one evil in place of another. Today, all that is far away, and who cares? Moreover, the human mania for judging and condemning impresses me as being an altogether comical one.

This story of mine, God knows, would be trite enough, if the hero of it were an athlete or a soldier. But beyond being a man of action, Hafner was a cerebralist. And that is the extraordinary thing. . . .

A cerebralist.

No art was foreign to him. I have seen his canvases; he painted enormous ones, full of mistakes and misconstructions, but overflowing with the pith of genius. A musician as well as a painter, his brush found amusement in attempting the absolute impossibility of translating Schumann into Rembrandt. And the disconcerting part *k* that he succeeded. And that nerve-racking thing, the Moonlight Sonata, Hafner also had hurled upon a living panel. And I swear to you that there was no necessity of writing the title under the painting. Not that it was good: it was worse, and it was exact. Only, the sallow color of the thing bored him; and one moody evening, he tore the canvas into bits, to make pieces for a game of patience.

He was a sculptor, as well. I have in my den a terra cotta, an Opium Woman, which he fashioned with his own fingers, and which serves me as mistress, now that I am weary of courting flesh-and-blood women. I believe that a fragment of his soul, of his first soul, remains in that opium-woman. I have said that he was a musician. He was a poet, too. An exquisite poet. Uneven, short-winded, but pure as a spring, and the author of many enchanting lines. . . .

I am acquainted with Pompeian friezes which are less luminous than his poems.

* * *

Such was Rodolph Hafner's first soul. And not for a moment during our three years of friendship,— three, or was it four?— not for a moment did his genius flag, not for a moment did his soul, replete with opium, sink back to the commonplace level of humanity. From day to day, I could see it growing, in wisdom and in subtlety. Indeed,—

It would be better not to write the rest. It is wise not to speak too lightly of the Drug. I know those who have not profited by doing so. For one thing is certain, and that is, that the Drug can do no wrong. When it bears some one ill will, there is a reason.

And that is none of our affair, yours or mine, shouldn't you
say? Yes, it would be better not to write it. But you would not
understand. . . .

Here it is, then. I am convinced that, from that day, Hafner's
second soul began to be born, or to be awakened in him. Yes,
that must be the way it came about. The second soul simply left
off sleeping. And probably, as I was telling you, that second soul
was nearer to being his than the first one, that wandering soul
which had lodged for a time in his vacant body. It was nearer
to being his own. One, then, was his legitimate soul, arid the
other a usurper. Jealousy. Hatred. Strife. Yes, strife, since the two
souls ended by battling each other,—by battling each other as
the Creoles had battled each other in the ring, mercilessly. I did
not witness this; I am supposing it. But the thing of which I am
certain is that it was that battle which exhausted Hafner's body.
. . . The ring, I remember, after the fight, was all trampled and
hollowed out, with dried red drops in the sand. . . . And Hafner's
body, similarly, some while before our separation, commenced
to be hollowed and withered, a good deal more quickly than was
natural at his age. There was less strength, less suppleness. His
exceedingly pale complexion became mottled with red,—like the
sand in the ring. The eyes grew fixed and feverish. The mouth
was white and parched. And then, his chest disappeared, and
there were only ribs to be seen, protruding under the skin. He
coughed, a hacking cough, which appeared to come from the
depths of his lungs. He became as thin as a lath, until he balanced
the scales at a truly laughable figure,—a mere child's weight.

One afternoon, in a public square, he climbed upon a pair of
scales, and a crowd flocked around him. That evening, I heard
him speak in his smoking-den for the first time. As he dipped the
needle into the opium, he murmured: "Dirty drug!" And after
smoking the first pipeful, he repeated, in a louder tone: "Dirty
drug!" I naturally thought that he was jesting. He was sick, that
was it. But why speak like that of opium? Opium never did any

one any harm, did it? Look at me; I get along very nicely, do I not? I would even go so far as to assure you that, if I had stuck to the Chinese pipes, there would have been no crannies in my brain. . . . No, Hafner was sick for the reason that his two souls were battling under his skin, battling with all their might, meanwhile trampling and laying waste his flesh, battling to see which would expel or slay the other. . . .

Finally, one morning, as he finished off the last pipeful, he rose and said to me: "Good-by."

I looked at him, without understanding.

"I'm going away," he said.

"But where?"

"Somewhere else."

And I never saw him again after that.

* * *

Never again, until yesterday. Yesterday, in the rue Blanche,— there is a smoking-place in that street,— what did I do but bump into a gentleman who was walking along with his nose in a newspaper. It was Rodolph Hafner.

He did not recognize me at first. Heavens, but I've grown older, I'm well enough aware of that. My cheeks now are hollowed, and I need a cane to walk with. But he,—he appeared to me to be still young, and yet changed. I took his arm. He was very happy.

"Ah, old man," he said, "what a lucky meeting!"

As he folded his newspaper, I saw that it was the *Petit Parisien*—the feuilleton.

"I have a lot of things to tell you, you know, after five years! I'm married, old chap. I have two sons!"

And he went on to tell me about his menage, his apartment, his wife's dowry and all about his youngsters. It was as though there were something incomparable, prodigious in all that. He also had a magnificent future. —"Since I've got down to business, you understand."— He had an income of twenty-five thousand from his embassy, and he would, one day, surely be minister plenipotentiary. As for me, I listened in amazement.

In front of the smoking-place, I said to him:

"You're going up with me?"

"Here?" he said, looking the house over.

"Yes, here, we'll smoke a few pipes together."

He leaped into the air like a goat. I thought he had gone mad. "Smoke opium!" he cried. "'Smoke opium! You want to kill me?"

Then he began a rambling speech.

It was I who was mad, *mad in wanting to smoke.* He never smoked any more. He was cured. Not without an effort, what the deuce! He had suffered martyrdom to get *the deadly poison* out of his system. Not to speak of the months and months that he had remained stupefied, beaten down, hovering between life and death. But little by little, he had got the upper hand. At thirty, one had something to fall back on, hadn't one? And he had taken on weight, too. Eighty kilograms, old top!

As for me, I had, already, a done-for face, and unless I wanted to croak at once, the best advice he could give me was to throw my pipes into the river,— as he had done.

I listened thoughtfully: the second soul. It was the second soul which had won the battle. There was nothing left of the first one.

I asked him questions. What about the genius he had shown, his painting, his music?

"Ah, old man, there's nothing to worry about in all that. I sent an entry to the Salon once, before my marriage. They turned me down, and they were jolly well right in doing so, you may be sure of that. A Bohemian trade, that of art. I never could have earned enough at it to butter my bread. Music, yes. That is always a pleasant pastime. Especially, cheerful music. As one grows older, one sees a lot of things more clearly. Schumann, Chopin—morbid bluffs. All that is no good for the nerves. And then, I write.

A little journalism doesn't do any one any harm. I play a little politics on the right side of the fence; and what do you think, it's won me the red ribbon!"

The second soul! The second soul! My God, what a tragedy! That other glowing, luminous soul,— where should I ever meet with it again?

I began to hate this Rodolph Hafner, who was so different and so vile a creature, in love with money, with bourgeois ambitions and with his belly, the enemy of poetry and of the ideal, the enemy of opium, the divine.

But he read none of this in my eyes. He understood nothing of my contempt.

"Rpn along," he was saying. "Poison yourself, if you've a mind to. That's none of my affair. But when you've had enough, think of me, old fellow. Look me over well. Am I strong, well set up and able to take care of myself or not? You can do the same thing. One pipe the less is one day more added to your life. And it's jolly good to be alive. Au re-voir. . . ."

He shook my hand and crossed the street. On the sidewalk opposite, he turned and called to me once more:

"You bet your life! It's jolly good to be alive!"

And then, he went off.

But at that very moment, a loosened slate fell from a roof and came tumbling down on his head. He dropped dead.

Quite dead. I crossed the street to make sure. The slate had bisected his cranium as clean as a stroke from a scythe. The second soul, driven out in its turn, had fled. All in all, a fitting revenge. Don't you think so?

The Sixth Sense

Sixteen, seventeen, eighteen? I no longer know. Have you noticed what an impossible thing it is to keep count of one's pipes? I no longer know how many I have smoked. . . . Let's see. My brain feels pliant and alert, while my forehead has become transparent. . . . This must be the twentieth, then. . . . My veins feel as though they were filled with an astonishingly light and lively fluid, which is certainly not blood, not the gross red blood of humankind. However, from the first puffs, I become obviously the superior of men,—nearer, in truth, to the gods. Yet this particular pipe must be the twentieth, seeing that the yoke of the sixth sense weighs me down less heavily now, from minute to minute; and very soon, I shall be the absolute equal of God,—pure spirit. The pity is that I am never able to rise from these mats, to materialize all the marvels which my brain incessantly is creating. For rise I cannot. It is even rather amusing, this extreme lightness of body, on the one hand, and on the other, this voluptuous paralysis which rivets one to the earth! The effect of the drug. I know of some very weird ones. . . .

"Mowg, will you smoke this? The next is mine. . ." No, the sixth sense is not yet absolutely atrophied. I shall need three or four pipes more. As I see Mowgli turning her throat toward me, her hips visible under the silk of her kimono, a temptation comes to me to enjoy that flesh. Four pipes, that would not be enough. For it is not enough to suppress desire; one must suppress even the appreciation of desire,—disembarrass the act of copulation of its prisms, and see it for what it is, as an inexplicable bit of clowning. Then only shall I be able freely to relish the quintes-

sence of my drunkenness,—and those pleasurable sighs which
come from the mats no longer shall be able to disturb my
serenity. You have smoked? Give me the pipe, so that I may
scrape the dross. This opium is too strong, it seems to me. . . .
They should have mixed the Benares with the Yunnan. . . .

Who are the smokers this evening? The lamp gives so wan a
light, and my eyes for so long have grown big with watching the
flame that I am no longer able to distinguish faces. Mowg, dear,
see to it that each one has his mat and his cushion, with a lamp
and a pipe not too far away. But reserve for my neck alone the
soft pillow of your belly. . . . Eh, what! The sixth sense is still
gnawing. Give, Mowgli, give to whom you like your body and
that flower of yours, —*since I no longer can make use of it;* but
save for me only your conjugal soul, your soul which is a twin to
mine, brought up like mine on opium. However lightly the years
may have flown for us, it has been a long time since we came
together as one. Here I am, thirty, while you are twenty-seven;
and not one day of quarrelling,—isn't that right, Mowg,—since
that first kiss of ours.

And yet, all this is very strange; and on certain days, I barely
can succeed in convincing myself of the truth of this life we have
led since our marriage. Especially, when the memory obsesses
me of the years that went before, of the time when I was a mere
lad, eager to live and bent upon squandering paternal millions
in the pursuit of pleasure. It is true, it is true! I was just that. It
is I who rode steeplechases on the fillies from my own stable;
it is I who crossed the Bay of Cowes on my racing-yacht; it is I
who fought on the Grande Jatte for Cendrelli's lips,—she who
was so beautiful in Isolde, and to whom I gave a thousand louis
each month. And here is something that is odder still: it is I who
am in love with the Miss Mowgli who is over there, whom I
impetuously married, giving up all pomps and all the works of
the devil, dreaming of nothing but her ingenuous mouth and the
chaste embrace of her cool arms. Miss Mowgli,—we selected

between us that pretty, savage name, and I afterwards forgot
your real one,—Miss Mowgli, daughter of the old admiral,
the victor of Formosa,—the barbaric little lass, barely out
of her convent, whose clear-seeing eyes seemed beyond the
reach of the whirlpools of sensuality. All that was one to me. I
remember our first modest nights, and the supreme intoxication
of kisses timidly given. . . . We traveled at first. Sailor ancestors
undoubtedly had given my loved one dimly sensed desires in
this direction. For one whole year, Japan held us under her
spell; and I can recall yet,—even now,—I can recall with gentle
fervor the silent ecstasies of her falling nights, as our yacht
crossed Simonoseki in the light of the setting sun. Yes, really, it
is possible that there was happiness upon the earth, at one time,
even for those who do not smoke. . . .

Mowgli, little loved one, do not turn away just yet. Without
fear of blackening your finger, make me up a pipe, in order that I
may be quickly ripe for your next treason. I can read very clearly
in that faithful soul of yours; and I am aware that you are merely
restraining your desire until the moment, soon to come, when I
shall be free of my churlish jealousy.

... It was later, in China, that the two of us smoked for the
first time. In China, at Shanghai, in Foochow Road. Oh! how
clear it all is in my head! The sixth of October, 1899,—eleven
o'clock at night. We had dined at a Chinese merchant's by
the name of Tcheng-Ta. When the singers had done with their
miauling, Tcheng-Ta suggested that, out of curiosity, we try
smoking a pipe in his den. Tcheng-Ta's den, in the body of the
building, which looked out upon an inner court. . . . On the walls
were four very obscene kakemonos, which caused Mowgli's
eyebrows to contract. But no sooner had I smoked a second pipe
than I forgot everything; I no longer perceived anything except
a miracle, mysteriously worked, and one which I always had
believed to be impossible: the clear eyes, the virgin eyes of the
companion of my journeyings grew large and hollow, then filled

with giddiness and sensual anxiety,—like eyes gazing into the depths of an abyss. And that evening, Mowgli, blunt and silent, sought my caress and breathed it in harshly between her closed teeth.

After that, we smoked every day.

. .. Mystery. The sixth sense awoke in her, at the same tinie that it became extinguished in me. . . .

We smoked every day. It is all very simple, is it not? Young, rich to the point of opulence, eager for all ennobling emotions that could give us life, we should have been fools, indeed, to refuse so noble an emotion as opium. Our souls, always very intimate, always sisters, always wed, at once came to under- stand each other better, became better gauged to each other. And now, our love is at its apogee. Our thoughts are identical and occur simultaneously, and we smile, dream and weep at the same instants, for the same reasons. But there is something more! While her body is abandoning itself to indifferent kisses, there, near me, in the smoking-room,—*I know* that her soul detaches itself to come and embrace my own, and it is thus that I discover my revenge for that moment of insignificant treason which she is powerless to prevent. . . .

What really has happened is this: the sixth sense has awakened in her flesh at the same time that it has gone to sleep in my own. There is nothing in all **that** which is in the least irrational, in the least abnormal, —though it may be incomprehensible. For that is the capricious,—no, the wise!— opium's sport. In women, who are creatures made for love, it provokes **and** increases amorous ardor; while in men, who are creatures made for thought, it suppresses that sixth sense which is coarsely opposed to cerebral speculations. There is no doubt that this is the way things come about, and that the opium is right,—the opium is always right.

... Another pipe.

The opium gradually has stripped me of my virility, has delivered me from that sexual obsession which is such a weight

for proud spirits and those truly eager for liberty. At first, fool
that I was, I was afflicted; and I rebelled, like the slave whose
chains are broken, and who basely regrets his master's bread and
roof. I blasphemed the opium's wise law, calling it *absurd* and
unjust. I could not understand how reasonable it was for desire
to cease to inhabit my man's flesh at the same time that it passed
over into the feminine flesh of my comrade. Stupidly, comically,
I wanted to go back upstream; I declined to abdicate my lover's
role,—until that wiser day when opium unsealed my eyes,—
unsealed her eyes,—until the day when our bodies became
divorced in order to permit our souls to share a more amorous
marriage,—in opium.

. . . One more pipe. Mowg, dear, patient one, it is the last.
I am free, now, of all. And I can feel your soul coquettishly
wheedling, beginning to skim my own with its provocative
kisses. Unbind, unbind your smarting body; hurl your fingers,
your throat, your belly to the nearest male, forgetful of a futile
modesty. Opium elevates us above the earth. I can see nothing
any more, except the black smoke which spreads magnificently
about the lamp; while I can hear a thousand marvelous
harmonies, which come to mask for me your sighs of joy, your
pleasurable outcries. Go on, laugh and weep, grip your evening's
lover in your avid arms, between your lascivious legs; madly
hurl him your lips, your teeth, your vibrant tongue; crush your
shuddering breasts upon his bosom. But as for me, I enjoy the
communion, a thousand times more intimate, of our blended
souls, along with a limitless wealth of ineffable caresses, of
unspeakable ardors. And not for a moment do I doubt that, if it
were not for opium, it would be my arms, my tongue and my
bosom now reveling in the possession of you. .. .

What is that? What is that name you call me, imbeciles? Oh!
what saddled beasts you are! Beasts!

FIFTH PERIOD
PHANTOMS

What Happened in the House in the Boulevard Thiers

WHAT HAPPENED in the house in the Boulevard Thiers, I shall not explain. And if I here set down what happened, it is with regrets. For so-called reasonable individuals will jest at it, while others, of whom I am one, will find nothing in the narrative to cure them of their madness.

I shall relate it, nevertheless, for the reason that it is true. It happened the first of May, last year, in a city, which I shall not name,—out of prudence. It happened on the fourth floor of a house that is neither old nor mystery-haunted, but newly built, ugly and unpretentious. This house had been erected quite recently, upon the rubbish of a disreputable section of the city. A wide boulevard overlooking the river, today replaces the hovels with closed shutters which formerly clung to the slopes of the cliff. The new quarter has an air of respectability; but it was the old stones, grown vicious from all the vice they had witnessed, which served as foundation for the new buildings. The Boulevard Thiers is, certainly, impregnated with the odor of lurking vice.

The house bears the number seven. It is a house given over to furnished lodgings. We occupied one whole floor, with eight or ten friends. I never was sure who the other tenants were. We had a smoking-den there, with rooms round about it. But no one slept in the rooms, for the reason that all preferred to smoke and talk until dawn, stretched out upon the rice-mats. For opium frees its followers from the yoke of sleep. On certain days, we amused ourselves with table-turning, finding sport in questioning the unknown force which exteriorized itself in our fingers, in order to lift the four legs, one after another. There was among us a singular chap, very young, quite beardless, with long flowing black hair. He was in the habit of dressing in the smoking-room, in a blue and yellow clown's costume, which he pretended was particularly suited to spirit-world experiences. As a matter of fact, he was a very middling sort of magician. The table turned readily enough under our hands, but nothing extraordinary ever happened as a result of it all.

Women frequently would visit us, eager for a taste of the kindly drug, eager also for caresses. For the sensitivity of women is so well padded and lined, during their black drunkenness, that a rude contact with men appears to them as delicate and docile a thing as contact with an androgyne. On the evening of which I am speaking, a girl of twenty had come in. We called her Ether on account of her passion; she needed each evening a full flask of sulphuric ether. That did not prevent her from smoking her fifteen pipes afterwards. On this evening, she was doubly drunk, and was sleeping nude. Some one caressed her lips. The wan lamp filled the den with half-shadows, as the rest of us talked, I no longer know of what.

How it was the fancy suddenly should have seized us to play at turning the table, it is impossible for me to recall. Hartus,—Hartus, the blue and yellow clown, with woman's hair,—was the first to rise, calling me over to assist him in carrying the table into one of the rooms;—for the table cannot turn in the presence ©f opium. Since I was slow in rising from the mats, he took the table and carried it himself. I can still see his bissected profile, as he bent over with the table resting against his stomach. For a minute, I remained stretched out, sulky at having to leave the gentle torpor of my sixth pipe. At my right, the unconscious Ether, intoxication heavy upon her head, was supporting with

her two hands a complacent mouth upon her body. I rose and followed Hartus.

In the damp, almost viscous room, he had lighted a solitary candle, the flame of which was dancing a saraband. Through the tulle curtains of the window-panes, the moon was sifting a hoar-frost over the walls. Seated opposite one another, our hands brushing the surface of the wooden table-top, we remained silent for some time. But something had gone wrong, for the table remained motionless. It did not even creak,—you know, those weird dry creaking sounds which precede the exteriorization of movement. No, something had gone wrong. We had already smoked, smoked rather well. That may have been the cause of it.

Finally, tired of the sport, I arose; and, the moon tempting me, I opened the window and leaned out on my elbow. I beheld the serenity of the night, the roofs drowned in whiteness, the river starred with reflection. It was very charming. A gentle breeze half-opened my pajamas and toyed with my bosom. In the absolute silence of that moment, I could hear the blue and yellow clown behind me blowing out the candle. And it was then that an inexplicable thing began to happen.

The breeze playing over my flesh seemed to me, suddenly, cold, very cold, as though the thermometer had dropped a dozen degrees. The table fell noisily and leaped up again. In the darkness, I fancied that Hartus had bumped against it and overturned it. But from the interior of the room, he immediately cried out to me not to make so much noise. I did not say anything; but I knew very well that I had not touched the table.

I was sufficiently frightened to contract my fingers over the window-ledge. Then, collecting my nerves by an effort of will, I turned back a step and stood facing the inexplicable phenomenon. The table was motionless, and Hartus was on his way to the smoking-room. I made a detour of the table, without daring to touch it, and followed him.

In the smoking-room, everything had remained in the state in which it was. Upon the mat, Ether continued to press her lover's lips against her flesh. The heavy curtains excluded the light of the moon. Only the solitary lamp was yellowing the ceiling of the room.

As I entered, Ether removed the man's mouth and nimbly arose. This surprised me greatly, for the moment before, ether and opium had held her completely paralyzed. *But she was no longer drunk now.* I could see her clear eyes, as she leaned against the partition, her hands at her throat. Her slender nudity impressed me as having grown and changed. Not in detail: I could recognize the round shoulders, the small rigid breasts, the narrow, feverish head. But the harmony of the whole was different. It was like coming upon a strange woman, chaste and haughty, with noble blood in her veins and rare thoughts in her brain,—no longer Ether, the courtezan, a washerwoman's illiterate daughter.—As I gazed upon her intently, I fell into a stupor. Her lover called to her, and she replied, in a slow-cadenced voice:

"Mundi amorem noxium horresco." *

She did not know how to read. She spoke only

French,—a passable sort of French, sullied with Breton idioms.

She continued, without interruption, in the same austere tone of voice,—the voice of a nun or an abbess:

"Jejuniis carnem domans, dulcique mentem pabulo nutriens orationis, Coeli gaudiis potiar" **

The smokers were not in the least astonished. To their dematerialized intellects, no doubt, that which I looked upon as extraordinary appeared as perfectly natural. The blue and yellow

---

* Guilty love makes me shudder.

** It is by conquering my flesh through fastings, and nourishing my soul on the gentle food of prayer, that I shall finally attain to the joys of Heaven.

clown, alone, arched his eyebrows and glanced at the woman.
Then, he remarked to her, with more politeness than was our
custom:

"Don't remain standing; you must be tired."

"*Fiat voluntas Dei! Iter arduum peregi, et affli-git me
lassitudo. Sed Dominus est praesidhim.*"*

He questioned her, curiously:

"Where are you from?"

She replied:

"*A terra Britannica. Ibi sacrifico sacrificium jus-titiae,
quia nimis peccavi, cogitatione, verbo et opere. Mea maxima
culpa*"**

The clown persisted in his questioning:

"What was your sin?"

"*Cogitatione, verbo et opere. De viro ex me films natus
est.*"***

I distinctly saw her white face turn red.

She went on, speaking always Latin, a mediaeval Latin, a
Latin of the convent and of the missal, which I understood only
by snatches,—the smell of opium assisting my memories of the
catechism.—I was near the lamp, and in the intervals between
words, I could hear the crackling of the drug on the ends of the
needles. That was the only thing which tempered my fear,—a
muffled fear, which parched my throat, and of which I was
unable to rid myself, despite the artlessness of the entire scene.
Hartus, emboldened by the pipes he had smoked and complete
master of his nerves, continued speaking without any show of

* May God's will be done! I have traveled a hard path, and I am very
tired. But God is my refuge and my strength.

** I come from the land of Britain. There I offer just sacrifices, for the
reason that I have sinned much, in thought, word and deed. The great fault is
mine.

*** In thought, in word and in deed. By man, of me, a son is born.

doubt. I looked at him, I looked at her, and the picture I have of
the two of them is so deeply inlaid upon my retina that no other
image ever shall be able to efface it.—I can see them now. He,
the blue and yellow man, crouched upon the mats, one hand
upon the floor, as the lamp at times turned his flowing black
hair to blond. She, the strange woman,—and surely, she was
strange!—nude, her back to the wall, her elbows crosswise,
her fingers interlaced under her throat. Words came and went
between them with a lively see-saw verve, as the room became
more and more impregnated with the atmosphere of the beyond. .
. . That strange voice preserved the monastic timbre it had had in
the beginning, but there was now greater strength behind it,—as
though it were drawing nearer. Mere phrases at first, desultory
and brief,—phrases uttered in haste, the phrases of a traveler
who is in a hurry, who has no time to talk,— expanding now into
more plenteous periods, swollen with incidents and flowering
with rhetoric. I understood no more, being a poor scholar and
too much beside myself.—Later, I questioned Hartus, who has
a knowledge of the tongue from seminary days. But he did not
answer. He does not like to speak again of those things.

I have preserved only the memory of that voice, that
Latinizing voice, gravely intoning what sounded like liturgical
responses. I caught certain words on the fly, the names of men
or of countries, or ecclesiastical terms, storing them confusedly
in my memory, without attributing to them then the sense
which I today discover in them,—wrongly discover, it may
be.—*Astrolabius, Athanasius, Sens, Argenteuil, ex-communitio,
concilium, monasterium.*—The voice grew animated and louder.
It was like a disputation, an oratorical conflict. Two words, out
of all the drift of phrases, remained floating upon the surface,
two words ten times repeated, with vehemence and with fury
at first, afterwards in a tone of grief and contrition:—*partem
supersubstantialem.* And then, suddenly, the voice paused,
saddened, infinitely saddened.

I then could hear the blue and yellow clown speaking, and although I knew nothing of what had been said up to then, his voice and question, alike, gave me the feeling of a hoax:

"Sin of lust? "What was God's punishment?"

The white face grew violently red, this time, and the voice dropped an octave. There was a solemn whispering, such as is heard in a confessional, and a few words barely reached my ears, with strange and repellent accents. ' I understood—*modo bestiarum— copulatione — membris asinorum erectis;* and violently uttered, as though vomited forth in disgust, was the word *castratus.* Having become calm once again, the voice slackened, to such an extent that the wording of the last phrase fixed itself in my memory:

"Fuit ille sacerdos et pontifex, et beatificus post mortem. Nunc Angelorum Chorus illi obsequantem concinit laudem celebresque palmas. Gloria Vatri per omne saeculum." *

"And you?" said Hartus.

"Dominus Omnipotens et Misericors Deus debita mea remisit. Virgo ego fatua. Sed dimissis peccafis meis, nunc ego sum nihil." **

She repeated, three times, the word: *"nihil."* And it seemed as though, of a sudden, she were speaking from a long way off. The last *"nihil"* was no more than a breath of sound.

The blue and yellow clown strode up to her, closely enough to reach out and touch her; and then, fastening his gaze upon those unflinching eyes, he called her "Heloise." The eyes closed in affirmation.

Then, he took her breasts in his hands and blew some opium into her face. She was motionless. But gradually, her muscles relaxed, and I could see tremors appearing upon her pallid face.

* He was priest and pontiff, and blessed after his death. The Angelic Choir is now singing his praises with palms. Glory-be to the Father forever.

** The Almighty and Merciful God has forgiven my sins. I was a foolish virgin. But now, my sins have been forgiven, and I am as nothing.

A minute more, and the eyes opened and capsized, the head and shoulders drooped, and upon the mats there remained now only a flaccid, lifeless form.

Then, her body slowly stirred, and from her mouth, that same mouth, there came another stammering voice, drowning in drunkenness.

"My Gawd! but it's cold! Hand me a pipe, will you? And now, my petticoat! I'm dying."

It is true, it was cold, cold as in a cellar.

One of the smokers thrust into a pipe-bowl the little brown ball which clung to his needle and extended the pipe to the one who had asked for it. It is possible that he, like myself, had heard. But no doubt the opium had shown him other and still more marvelous visions.

The Cyclone

THE ONE who saw the vision told me of it. And I know many other things that are stranger still. But they would not appear strange to you, who are not smokers. Your intelligence, not having been sharpened by opium, would look upon them as simple and normal occurrences. And so, I shall tell you of nothing except the vision.

The one who saw it is neither a liar nor insane, for he is a smoker. Opium dissipates earthly illusions and enforces sincerity. As for myself, I do not smoke, on account of an oath. But every night, I stay up in a smoking-den, and I go to sleep upon the mats as a lurid dawn enters through the air-hole and turns the lamp-light yellow. And the black smoke which is then heavy round about us ends by penetrating my brain, bringing with it a little light and a little candor.

I shall, then, merely repeat what he told me, without altering a single word. On that evening, we were lying in the smoking-room as usual. Not alone, for opium loves gatherings of the faithful. There were two women upon the mats. As for one of them, her name is not to be set down here, for the reason that she is what is known as a respectable woman; it is in secret that she comes to smoke with us, and her husband, who has a run upon a steamer, knows nothing of it. The other one we will call Joujou, for the reason that she permits herself to be used as a plaything by many men. In the street, to be sure, these two women would look with contempt upon each other, by reason of their different stations in life, but in the presence of opium, the great leveler, they are friends, and frequently are to be seen slumbering in each other's arms.—Upon the mats were three young fellows who had come to flirt with opium. They smoked little, spending their time in caressing the women. Their intertwined bodies could be vaguely made out by the wan glow of the lamp. They, perhaps, did not hear, and who knows if they remember? He smoked, and I watched him as he made up his pipes, breathing in the black spirals and emitting them through his mouth.

But I have not told you who he is. The truth is, I know nothing of his age or what he looks like, since when I saw him, he was always reclining upon the mats, and the lamp-light was very dim. His beard, however, is silver and his eyes are of a green-metallic luster. We call him the Silent, for the reason that he never speaks until after the third pipe, when he gives utterance to some extraordinary remarks. He has seen all countries, and opium has made it possible for him to understand them. I believe he is the captain of a man-of-war, but I am not sure; what takes place outside the smoking-room is no concern of mine.

This, then, is what he told me, one night when we had spoken for a long time of visions and of phantoms:

"The most sinister are not those which wander about in cemeteries, or those which lie in ambush in haunted houses, in order to pounce upon and strangle incredulous dunces. "We all have seen that sort, we smokers. They do not dare raise a hand against us, for they are very well aware that opium renders us quite as fluid and immaterial as they themselves, and that we can scent them in the night more quickly than they can scent us. But I have seen others, which are not concerned with the living, for their business as phantoms weighs too heavily and too terribly upon them.

". . . Tell me, do you, by any chance, remember the *Renard?* No? That happened many years ago, in the days when seven rather full pipes were enough to make me drunk. And now, I need forty. The *Renard* was a cruiser which, in some unknown fashion, met with shipwreck. It was a long slender ship whose hull scarcely seemed to rest upon the water, and whose three very tall masts seemed to be fleeing the black waves. Well, the *Renard* put out, one fine calm day, and never came back. In its stead came a cyclone, which laid waste the seacoast. And this cyclone was not like other cyclones; it whirled from right to left, whereas its brothers of the Indian Ocean invariably whirl from left to right. That always impressed me as being a weird sort of thing; but I thought no more of it at the time. Except that one day, in a Tonkinese smoking-den, a Dutchman assured me that there was such a thing as a special kind of tempest,—living tempests, which were to be recognized by the fact that they violated all natural laws, blowing from the north, when they should blow from the south, going to the right when one expected them on the left—doing everything, in short, in a topsy-turvy fashion. Those tempests, he explained to me, are the manifestations of evil and occult spirits, and they are the most dangerous of all for ships.— And he had a variety of stories to tell me on that score.

"As for myself, I listened to what he had to say, and fell to thinking that the cyclone which struck the *Kenard* must have been one of those living ones. But I did not give the matter much thought, otherwise.

"For one thing, no one was any longer concerned with the *Kenard.* The wives of those on board had first taken and then abandoned the black robe and the crepe veil. A number of them had remarried, which probably did not bring them a great deal of luck. In short, the years had slipped by. How many, I no longer know; for the pipes prevent one from taking note of the flight of time.—I say, should you mind lowering the lamp a little; the flame has scorched this pipeful. . . ."

He was silent as I adjusted the wick. And then, we heard a gentle, panting wail from the mats. One of the women was in the throes of love; which one, I do not know, for the reason that he, by that time, had taken the opium on the end of his needle,—and

I preferred to watch the drug as it grew yellow and inflated above the flame.

He went on, then, his phrases scanned by the woman's voluptuous sighs, coming in like the accompaniment of a lute:

"Yes, every one had forgotten the *Renard,* myself among the rest. Not a scrap of news, and for so long a time! There was only one proof that the ship had been lost, but that was a very definite sort of one: a shattered plank which a fast-sailer had fallen in with at sea, a plank from the rear breastwork on which the letters RENA.. could still be distinguished, the other letters having been torn away. There was no longer any room for doubt, since all the seamen had recognized the letters on the plank.

"And then, one day, I took it into my head to go to China, since the opium the druggists sell here is worthless, and I felt the need of another brand. I left upon a big cruiser whose name I do not care to tell you, since she brought me bad luck. For in the Indian Ocean, a cyclone swooped down upon us.

"They had warned us of it at Aden. The cyclone's approach had been flashed ahead by cable. But being pressed for time, we had set out, anyway. The commandant assigned me the task of calculating the tornado's orbit, which, as you know, is not a difficult thing to do. I made my observations, drew up my figures and turned in my papers on the evening of the second day out. Having done this, I retired to my cabin and, under lock and key, started in to smoke.

"At first, all went well, and I smoked until nightfall. More and more of a sea was coming up all the while, but upon my mat, the rock of the boat was not annoying.

"But as night fell, I felt, all of a sudden, that something abnormal was happening. What? I had no idea. But I scented something of the unknown, of the supernatural, and *that something was coming nearer to us.* At that moment, the taste of the opium appeared to me to undergo a change. It seemed to me that the smoke was as impressed and as disturbed as I. However,

I kept on smoking, as the night all the while grew blacker. There was now no longer any light coming in through the porthole.

"As I continued smoking, the sensation became more precise. The opium, decomposed as it had been by the thing's approach, continued, nevertheless, to cast a light about my head. One by one, a number of certitudes came to me. First, *that of a double danger.* Why double? I had no intimation; but I was quite sure that two equally mortal perils were bearing down implacably upon us, and I also felt that *they were whirling perils.* In my mind, the association was then complete; I thought of the cyclone. But at the same time, I felt that the whirling *was from right to left.* My calculations, in that case, had certainly been at fault. But I did not waste much time over that; for I at once knew that my calculations were of small importance, and that we were not dealing with any ordinary cyclone.

"And then, suddenly, a horrible thing happened to me; the lamp was completely, and for no reason at all, extinguished, and the darkness filled me with terror. I could hear the cabin furniture groaning and the fibers of my mat crunching with fright. The howling of the wind pierced the walls and swept over me. And I understood, very clearly, that this was no natural wind, a simple, more or less furious displacement of air, but rather, a living thing, one capable of intellection and of thought, and which undoubtedly, at that very moment, was asking itself the question as to whether or not it should crack to pieces the little nutshell that we were.

"I was drunk, and my legs shook under me. However, I arose with a leap; and clinging to the stairs, I made my way up on deck. The wind was so strong that I scarcely could hold on.

"I had just reached the top of the ship's ladder, when the wind suddenly sank, as at the voice of Christ. There was no doubt that we were in the center of the tornado; and you are aware that there is always a calm at the center. In spite of this fact, it is the most dangerous of all places, for the reason that the wind is there whirling at a dreadful rate of speed.

"No matter. In this factitious calm, I had a chance to get my sea-legs and stagger over to the gunwale. And it was then that I saw the vision.

"Upon the surface of the tremendously phosphorescent water, which was like a shroud quilted with an infinite number of golden drops,—upon the water, a ship was riding beside us.—A long, slender ship, whose hull seemed scarcely to rest upon the sea, and whose three very tall masts appeared to be fleeing the world of the living. They shimmered, those masts, as reflections shimmer upon the water, and their tops were lost in the sky like smoke. The hull, on the other hand, was outlined with extraordinary precision, more precisely than any hull of wood and steel. And upon the deck, men were distinguishable, with blanched faces and sparkling gilt upon their uniforms. All these objects, however, were quite opaque, and through planks and men I continued to behold the sea and its phosphorescences.

"The phantom-vessel passed us without my hearing the sound of its engines. It whirled slowly upon itself. As the stern passed near me, I could see the breastwork, from which one plank was missing; two letters of the ship's name alone remained, and they were the lost two: .... RD.

"It disappeared, then, in the distance. The wind began puffing again, more violently than ever, and I could make out no more. Evidently, the center of the living cyclone was dragging with it, into infinity and into eternity, the ghost of the dead ship.—As for me, I went below and started to smoke again. But the opium had turned like milk, and the pipes were all stale. And that was what frightened me the most. —Pass me the sponge; my bowl is all dirty."

He was silent. Upon the mats, both of the two women were now groaning under the weight of caresses, and their ardent sighs were mingling with one another. But I,—I merely watched the pipe, as it grew brilliant once again, under the friction of the little water-imbued sponge.

Out of the Silence

No, rr is not yet night. I had thought that it was night. But not yet. The fact is, I cannot see well any more. As soon as I am intoxicated, a veil of mist falls in front of my eyes, a brown, wavering, undulating veil. Through this veil, I distinguish objects with difficulty, and it seems to me that they vacillate and assume double shapes. It is very funny. I keep on smoking, and the smoke from the pipes puffs out enormously and becomes opaque, exactly like the foul smoke from steamer stacks,—the disgusting smoke of the steamboat which carried me away from my wept-for Tonkin.... Bah! I don't even think of that any more.

No, it is not night. What luck! An hour yet, it may be, an hour in which to go on living, satisfied and reassured, in the clamorous solitude of day. For the day is filled with noise. Filled with bustle and with tumult, even in the heart of this lost land, even in the absolute isolation of my fumerie, in the absolute isolation of my own house, in the absolute isolation of my cemetery, far from village and from farm, far from the last human hovel. The people here do not come near the cemetery; they are afraid of it; no one among them was willing to be the sexton, and so, they had to come looking for me,—me, the old sergeant of the legion, who was dying of hunger on the streets of Paris. I was quite willing to look after it, for my part. I'm not afraid of the cemetery. I'm not afraid. . . .

Is that the night dropping down? No, it must be the smoke from this pipe. Hell of a pipe! There is too much dross in it; the bamboo is all black... . Just the same, I'm going to shut the gates this minute. ... I prefer to go down there before nightfall . . . before twilight, even.—I am going down there.

* * *

There, I've locked up. Good God! what a racket in this sunny cemetery! I'm deaf with it. There are bees, and there are dragon-flies, with their fluttering and their humming. There are birds, also, with their calls and twitterings, and the air is heavy with reduplicated echoes. And then, the trees, and the shrill wind which rumples their leaves, and the mad rustling of crickets and grasshoppers: in short, so many great and startling sounds,—now sharp, now deep,—but all deafening. Not counting the distant sonorities which come to me, relentlessly: farm beasts, peasants at labor, and the factory in the neighboring village, barely five leagues distant.... Oh, I hear them, right enough! And all together, they prevent me from divining those other noises,—slight, murmuring, low-voiced noises,—the noises of the night, awaiting their turn. ... It is not yet night, hey?

It's all the same. But one thing is sure, and that is that I did not use to hear so many sounds.

It is the opium. It is as though I had had wax in my ears and the warm smoke had melted it. I recall the days of my youth and, later, the days when I was a soldier in the Sud-Oranais and the Sahara. In those days, I could hear no better than other men. The desert was mute, and the mystery of its sands filled the silence, from the moment dawn had driven the nocturnal jackals back to their lairs. Filled with silence likewise, in the olden days at the hour of noon, was my native village, graying on the slopes of the brown Cevermes; and in the evening, over the rocky hills, over the valleys with their scant pasturage, over all the moors, entangled with pines and heather, there was even more of silence, that sovereign silence which dropped down with the night. . . .

Old wives' tales! It is a fine story that *I do not hear it any more, the silence.* That is a dream, a myth,—a Utopia. The Utopia of dumb brutes and beasts of burden. The Utopia of those who do not smoke. There is no more silence.

All this began at Tonkin, when I first started smoking. Yes, upon my word, right away. I remember my arrival down there, on the deck of the transport. "We had put in at Saigon; and in the evening, those on leave had been turned loose in the city. Like the others, I thought only of drinking-bouts, gluttonies and women. But no sooner had I left the gang-plank than I stopped short before a large wall that skirted the first street. There came from behind it an odor that I never had smelled before, a gentle and disturbing odor,—an odor which, from the very first, made its way through my nostrils to my soul, thus completing my subjugation. I did not as yet even know what the drug was. Nevertheless, I proceeded to forget everything else, and I remained there until dawn, my back to the wall,—to the wall of the opium-shop, —inhaling and sniffing with all the breath I had. And little by little, in the silent darkness, I could hear from far away, very far away, too far away, the laughter of my comrades, engaged in forcing in the doors of brothels. . . .

Afterwards came my first pipe, at Pak-Nah, in the frightfully distant little post on the edge of the mountain-forest, the forest of mystery, filled with dead and rotting leaves which begot fever and madness. We smoked a lot down there. And at night, we could very plainly hear the roving tigers, even though they sought to tread the brushwood with a footfall lighter than that of cats. It was rather amusing at first, those imperceptible noises which we, none the less, infallibly detected. One evening, a pirate from Doc-Theu's band came to spy on the post. He slipped in along the palisades without any more noise than an adder; but we heard him, all the same, and our hearing was so precise that, just as he went to climb the bamboos, my own corporal put a bullet in his belly, by guess-work, without even seeing his man. Another night, the post bell sounded, and we sharpshooters clacked our teeth, being convinced that one of the forest genii was thus warning us of the imminent death of our outfit. But my ear, as it happened, while the bronze was still tingling, had already caught the tramp of our nanny-goat's hoofs; having broken her tether, she had ducked her head and run full-tilt against the bell-rope.

Yes, all that was perfect. It was afterwards that I found less to admire in the matter.

Oh, at first, the inconveniences were slight enough. Rather comical than otherwise. In the Tonkin outposts, where I lived far from humankind, I quickly came to know and recognize the host of silent noises that I heard. Later, in France, at Paris, I heard other sounds, not quite so simple,—human sounds. . . . From the day of my arrival in the little hotel where I put up, it was minutely enervating, the moving in and out of each guest in each room,—the one who snored, and the one who made love, and the one who left the water running in his wash-basin. . . . Then, I found lodgings at the other end of Mont-parnasse,—a lifeless quarter, which I had picked expressly for that reason.—It was well chosen! From die very first day, I could hear all the night-hawks, aH the forced locks, all the fences that were scaled,— just as, in the old days, at Pak-Nah, I had heard the pirate legging it over the palisade. And I would dig my finger-nails into my bed-clothes, constantly expecting to see my door open and some brigand come stalking in, who would have to be received with blows of a cudgel.... And so, I moved. I sought lodgings then in the heart of Paris, in the faubourg Saint-Antoine. Merely a shift of scene this time. The racket was such,—day and night,—that I was no longer able to distinguish one noise from another. It was like a formidable orchestra with all the instruments howling and screeching in unison. The only result was, I did not sleep at all; for opium is not so great a friend of sleep as that! I no longer slept at all, and I was up against it. As a climax, my supply of opium was already running low. I had brought with me all that I was able to carry; but to begin with, those dirty customs-officers had stolen a box from me; and in the second place, I had figured that I would smoke less in France than I had smoked down

there, whereas the contrary was the case. I ended by finding an
obliging druggist in Paris, but the brand he carried was nothing
but rubbish, and what was more, my nine-hundred-sixty-five
francs of pension-money were going fast. They had promised
me, in all good faith, a tobacco-shop,—I limp a little, ever since
my wound at Son-Tay,— but it was, as usual, a curate's son who
got it! Then, I applied for the post here, and became the sexton of
the cemetery.

There you are; it's night now. I can hear the bats beginning
their shaggy flight. I thought, I had heard the birds sounding a
retreat. And now, the wind has dropped. That caps the climax.

"What you do not know is that I can also hear, at night, this
cemetery of mine. There are other noises now, not so clear, not so
simple, not so candid as the noises of day;—but more dangerous
to listen to, more agonizing, more torturing. At first, I thought
it was the dead slipping out of their sepulchers to do a skeleton-dance in the moonlight. But no, it is not that. The dead are
dead, and do not come back. Or if they do come back, it is with
footsteps so furtive that I do not hear them,—not even I!—*not
yet.*—No, I cannot hear the skeleton-dance. I hear something
else. . . .

I hear forbidden sounds, sounds which no one has ever
heard,—the pallid and macabre sounds which lie stagnating at
the feet of cypress-trees and of mausoleums,—those nocturnal
sounds which are afraid of the sun, of the living breeze and of the
songs of birds;—those cold sounds which freeze the flesh of men
and cause the hair to bristle upon their skins. I hear the creaking
and the moaning of cof-finwood, under the viscous humidity
of the rain-soaked earth. I hear caskets which are too heavy,
gradually sinking into the slimy mud, sinking eternally. I hear
rotten flesh swarming with nimble vermin, and the clattering of
dried bones as they subside, one after another, upon the cloth of
winding-sheets. And this square walled enclosure where fifteen-
hundred corpses have come to sleep, one after another,—fifteen-

hundred terrifying noises escape from it and come gliding, every
night, to my too finely attuned ears,—fifteen hundred groans
from the beyond, each one of which insinuates its grain of
madness into my ruined brain.

There you are. My opium-lamp alone is left to yellow my
walls. Not a single reflection of twilight longer enters through my
shutterless window. Down there, I can hear the will-o'-the-wisps
grazing the little yews. It is night, black night. Hey, is that the
coffins moaning? Do you hear them?

My God, yes, I'm sure of it! I should have left this noisy
cemetery. But I cannot. Where would I find opium, opium
which keeps me alive, magic opium, which intoxicates me with
delicious illusions, intrepid opium, which supports me here,
trembling but true to my post, in defiance of vagrant madness?
Where? It is the cemetery which gives it to me.—It is true,
though I have not told you, that black poppies grow everywhere;
but it is only in Yunnan,—and in India, as well,—that opium
oozes from it as drops of honey do from the wax of hives. It
was in vain that I endeavored to manufacture opium in France,
—down to the day when my Tonkinese poppies, planted in the
corpse-fattened cemetery, marvel-ously recovered their original
virtue; now, the moment I make an incision in the sugar-swollen
heads, brown drops pearl out to my heart's content; and when
I have rolled all the agglomerated drops into one big ball, and
when I have dissolved the pellets in the water of my kettle,—
when I have filtered them, when I have heated them, when I have
reduced them,—Ah, then, my smooth black opium is worth all
the drugs of Benares and of China. And it is the cemetery which
has worked the miracle. So, you can see plainly enough that I am
in no position to leave it. . . .

Hey! I heard. . . . No, I did not hear.

I did not hear. It is not true that a louder creaking has gushed
forth from the mortuary soil. It is not true that a coffin has sunk
down into its bed. It is not true that a jolted board—is still
gnashing terrifically against its inexorable nails.

Because if it were true, that would be the sixth one buried alive to agonize in my cemetery,—the sixth one this year,—the sixth, one after another, to whose groans and death-rattle I have had to listen,—the sixth one gradually to expend his moribund efforts against the wooden solidity of his casket,—the sixth whom I have heard mangling his feeble hands—with his teeth,— and dying, dying of fear and of despair. Yes, I have undergone this atrocity five times within a year ... and I shall have to endure it one time more, for the reason that,—of what use to lie?—It is true: the one buried alive is stirring, and I can hear his anguished sigh, close neighbor as yet to the lethargic sleep from which he is awaking. . . .

Ah, yes? So, you think, my good folks, that this does not happen, that it is a pure invention on the part of the sick or of the romancer, that tombs are always passive, and that there is no such thing as persons buried alive? You foolishly believe, upon the word of solemn *morticoles,* that contemporary science never makes a mistake, and that it never buries any but corpses? Go on counting on that, and sleep in peace, *you who can.* As for me, to whom opium has given ears with which to hear, I hear. And I know that, out of every ten who are buried, there is one who is not dead. And I also know that this one's agony,—his second agony,—surpasses in horror all that your poor obtuse brain could possibly imagine. It may be that you will admit another stu- pid assumption on the part of the medicasters; it may be, you believe that the old codger who, in a lethargy, is stuck six feet underground, never more than half awakes, and that he at once parts again with both sense and breath, after he has barely suc- ceeded in laying hold of them for a moment. Ah! so you think so! Then, you do not know what life is, and with what claws a dying man clings to it, when he feels it escaping him? At Tonkin, in the old days, I used to hunt deer,—big, tawny deer, with for the reason that,—of what use to lie?—It is true: the one buried alive is stirring, and I can hear his anguished sigh, close neighbor as yet to the lethargic sleep from which he is awaking. . . .

Ah, yes? So, you think, my good folks, that this does not happen, that it is a pure invention on the part of the sick or of the romancer, that tombs are always passive, and that there is no such thing as persons buried alive? You foolishly believe, upon the word of solemn *morticoles,* that contemporary science never makes a mistake, and that it never buries any but corpses? Go on counting on that, and sleep in peace, *you who can.* As for me, to whom opium has given ears with which to hear, I hear. And I know that, out of every ten who are buried, there is one who is not dead. And I also know that this one's agony,—his second agony,—surpasses in horror all that your poor obtuse brain could possibly imagine. It may be that you will admit another stu-pid assumption on the part of the medicasters; it may be, you believe that the old codger who, in a lethargy, is stuck six feet underground, never more than half awakes, and that he at once parts again with both sense and breath, after he has barely suc-ceeded in laying hold of them for a moment. Ah! so you think so! Then, you do not know what life is, and with what claws a dying man clings to it, when he feels it escaping him? At Tonkin, in the old days, I used to hunt deer,—big, tawny deer, with tapering legs;—well, one day, I emptied two chambers of my Lebel into a poor female who had fallen stiff, her whole breast torn away.—I easily could have put my two fists into the hole. I came up to her and placed my foot upon the red carcass,— and the carcass rose and trotted off, dragging after it bowels, heart and lungs! They are like that, these ones I am telling you of, who are buried alive. Very nearly as dead as their neighbors, the skeletons, they still howl at the top of their voices and keep turning over, in order to strain their backs against the coffin-coverings! Listen, listen, do you hear that gnashing plank? Fortunately, the earth is heavy above him. He will not succeed in getting out, the bugger! I shall never see him, all pale and begrimed with thick mud, galloping madly away among the tombstones. Fortunately!

Come, another pipe! Good God, how long the night is!

The Red Palace

ONE THING is certain: I am no longer a man, no longer a man at all.

Of that, there can be no doubt. There is no longer anything in common between myself and the human race,—no longer anything, neither sense nor thought. It is clear that life,—for I can see, and that is the para-doxical part of it!—it is clear that life functions in me by essentially different springs, and such as give rise to vital phenomena under an altogether novel and superior form. I am, then, no longer a man. But,—and this is surely a unique circumstance!—I have not become anything else.— Neither corpse nor ghost.—Nothing at all. My body is there; I look upon it, and I touch it; it is the body of a man, true enough. In order to achieve their present formation, there was no need of my sense and thought's leaving it. Why, I even have preserved my former appear ance, and those who were my kind might be deceived thereby. I have broken with the earth, but without setting foot in the beyond. And, on the other hand, I scarcely may be said to be a soul in pain, tossed about in the interregnum between two stages,—something like a child, already cast off by the maternal belly and not yet brought to the light of day.—How ever weird all this may seem, I am in no wise aston ished by it. In short, what has happened is, simply, this: my ego has ripened too quickly,—in advance of its proper season,—and that is all there is to it. I recall having seen, once, a barn on fire in the middle of an orchard. It was in the springtime. From eve ning to morning, the peaches and the apricots grew heavy and vermilion, having

been ripened by the fire; and yet, they did not fall, for the reason
that the branches which bore them had remained green. And so
it is with my body, which has remained alive about me,—about
me,—me, who am dead,—who have been born into the superior
life of the here after.

No, really, I am not in the least surprised by it all. For,
when one reflects upon it, what reason is there for an obligatory
simultaneity in the death of the two,—the death of the being
and the death of the wrapper? None whatsoever. The wrapper
may at tain its second existence, putrescence, while the being,
still young and uncultivated, remains wholly unfitted for the
beyond.—And reciprocally. Nothing is more likely or more
logical. Any accident is sufficient to bring such a thing to pass:
a pebble in the road, some imperceptible cause,—the fire which
ripened the peaches,—the opium which, patiently, pipe by pipe
ful, I have come to substitute for the blood in my veins. For I
have smoked my weight in opium in the course of -my life,—and
more than that, since my ego died. Opium was the cause with
me. The life of my being was accelerated and cut short, while the
organic life of my bodily wrapper continued to pursue its normal
course of evolution.

Nothing, I say again,—nothing is more likely, no-thing is
more logical. Opium the immaterial, opium the prodigious, might
very well, at will,—might it not?—raise a man above all other
men and absolutely disengage him from his grosser substance,—
through deterioration, as the case might be, through the ruin or
through the suppression of that substance. That is somewhat the
case with me. My body is living, yes, but not intact; opium has
been able to emaciate it and attenuate it sufficiently to prevent its
encumbering me further,—and to render the beyond accessible
to me. And I am more gratified over the result than were those
ascetics who, by means of a hair-shirt dis cipline,—a barbaric
and a puerile process,—succeeded in half-conquering their
roaring senses. What a long time it has been since my own senses
entered the void!

And yet, my body, diminished, atrophied, ampu tated, goes on living! There it is; I can see it, and I can touch it. By means of it, I preserve a tether to the earth. It is the firmament of humankind that I behold, blue for me as for them, and dotted with white stars. It is the salt sea which plashes the sides of my boat, while the spray from the oars make me shiver with the cold. I can hear the boatman singing, and his song, melodious to human ears, is not displeas ing to my own. I really would seem to be a man still.

* * *

There is the bank, and the stone stair leading to the quay. Behind me, the Boghasi indulges in its nightly plaint, and gnaws eternally at the two continents it separates. In front of me, the Red Palace, deserted and in ruins, cuts off the horizon with its blood-red bulk.

At the gate, the sentinel leans heavily on his musket, the red of his fez blending with the wall. One does not enter here, under pain of death. But I have given the sentinel,—who is a smoker,—some opium, and the free-masonry of the drug is a bond between us. He does not see me as I pass. Here I am in the antechamber, under the great beams which, gnawed through by age, will soon come tumbling down,—now, on the stair covered with mats, with used mats which have turned to dust;—now, in the high-ceilinged rooms, from which one perceives, at the rear, a park in the form of an amphitheatre;— and now, under the roof, where my fumerie is.

It is but a rug,—an old Bokhara, forgotten in its garret,—a smooth copper tray, a black bamboo pipe and a lamp which smokes from under its mended glass. The walls are of bare wood, and the paint on the rafters is peeling. But through the window which has no glass, the park, forty times a centenar ian, freely confers its formidable majesty.

And no sound comes, save the sighing of the wind, torn by the pointed branches of the dead trees.

Here I am now, reclining upon my left side, as I hastily prepare my first pipe.

* * *

The Red Palace is an ancient dwelling, built by no one knows whom. Many masters have inhabited it, and nearly all of them have there died a tragic death. An evil destiny wanders about its walls and goes into hiding near the gates, under the all too thick foliage of the park.

A prince once made it his residence,—a Greek prince, celebrated in history; his name signifies trea-son.—In those days, the Red Palace was full of luxury and magnificence. Slaves of all races thronged it, and very noble visitors came there to greet its master, arriving on admirals' galleys with fourteen rowers each.

The prince was an old and a powerful man. Age and pride had forged for him a heart of steel. Frequently, for slight cause, he would condemn his servants and his eunuchs to the worst of punishments. Heads fell under the scimitar, until the terrace of the park came to be soaked in blood.

And I happen to know that this blood was there mingled with vestiges of other and more ancient blood, a horrible blood which had been spilled upon this same terrace so many centuries before that no one any longer was able to remember.

One evening, certain mutes crossed the threshold. They were under the command of one who bore a green parchment, at the sight of which all genu flected. The prince, rudely seized in his own room, offered no resistance, and even kissed the august signature. And there, to that nail in the rafter, a rope was fastened, and the prince was hanged from it. When the violet-colored tongue had slipped out from between the bloodless lips, when the great toes had ceased their convulsive contractions, the execu tioners cut the rope, and then cut off the head to bear it to their sovereign. For three days, the decapitated body remained without sepulture,—here, upon this very floor-plank. The slaves, frightened out of their wits, had fled. And it was a woman, come from none knew where, who furtively buried the cadaver, down there in the park, at the foot of the big spindle-wood tree,—on the very spot where, a hundred years later, another woman buried the body of a dog.

Since then, the Red Palace has known other mas ters. But there was not one among them who slept without fear, and misfortune came to many of them. The sovereign himself, whose seal upon a piece of green parchment had dared to cross the ominous threshold and assume command under that perilous roof,—that sovereign had his somber morrow. De posed by his own people, he died strangled in a dungeon. His Empire, for long centuries a brilliant and a glorious one, foundered in shame and in blood. Bellicose peoples assailed it from all sides, and princes wearing the aureole of Destiny shared the spoils. And now, the Imperial Standard, derisive rag that it is, feebly waves over a few uncultivated fields, a few desert strands, a few dismantled forts,—despicable fragments which the conquerors did not want.

And the Red Palace, henceforth crumbling and empty, the mysterious Red Palace, is only waiting for the Empire's last agony, before sinking at last into dust.

.. . Yes, I am no longer a man, no longer a man at all. But I have not yet become anything else.

I am, thus, in the middle of the bridge, equally dis-tant from one bank and from the other. And surely, no one can go on living in the middle of a bridge. One must go on, or go back.

To go back, to become a man once more,—I do not even think of that. For to be precise, I am dead. I should, then, have to be resurrected. A thing clearly impossible. To be resurrected, to go back, I cannot and I will not.

Go on, that is what I must do. But go on, what is that? To become,—to become what? To become a ghost, how? By slaying myself,—that is to say, by slaying my body? But that process, rude and repel-lent, is anything but sure. Can I be certain as to what would be the result of my physical death? Is it wise thus to risk, upon a throw of the dice, that tremendous portion, the one portion that is my own? Surely not. First of all, one should not undo what one cannot reestablish.

I ought not to kill myself, then.

But, granted that, I am still in the grip of uncer tainty.

The better course is, it naturally follows, to wait,— to wait, even though the waiting be extremely diffi cult and fatiguing,— to wait and to smoke.

And so, if I am here in the Red Palace on this eve ning, following so many other evenings, it is not with any purpose of unraveling the Gordian knot that holds me bound,—since I am not yet able to un ravel that knot, and since I dare not cut it. No, it is merely to wait, and to smoke.

Opium, moreover, is the only sedative my anxiety knows, since it alone is able to bring men near to phantoms, and to remove that opaque veil which separates the here from the hereafter. Up to this moment, it has not seen fit to undo the knot for me, —to make me a phantom. But every night, it ren ders visible and intangible, to those new senses which it has given me, beings of the other world, of that world to which I soon shall belong. Thanks to opium, I taste the exile's dolorous joy, as he contemplates from the altitudes of his island the shoreline of his fatherland

This pipe is the thirtieth, so nearly as I am able to reckon. That is sufficient to unseal my eyes. And now, as I look out into the park, I begin to see less clearly the bushes, the clusters of foliage and the lin dens on the terrace, stretching out toward the black sky their branches which are like twined serpents; less clear, also, are the imprecise, discolored and wavering forms which glide here and there through the night-mist. . . .

Opium does not call up phantoms. On the con trary, its dark and sovereign power frightens them away. I know that the black smoke which now spreads over my rug is sufficient to protect me from fantastic attack of any kind. The frail apparitions

which wander about in the park never would dare cross this
window-sill,—never. But, thanks to opium, the intrepid and
the clairvoyant, I can see them, and so, am able to stroll freely
through my fatherland-to-be.

And that is why it is, I have chosen the Red Palace as an
asylum. That is why it is that, each evening, I laboriously
drag my tired limbs here, the tired and sorrowing limbs of a
smoker who is never satisfied. Where, better than in this blood-
bespattered dwell ing, with its roof of masonry,—where should I
be better able to come upon those visions which are now the sole
diversion that my dead being knows?

* * *

Phantoms are in the habit of wandering near those places where
their cadavers have reposed. The Red Palace, a terrible and a
lamentable necropolis, swarms with pale and weeping ghosts.

This is my sixtieth pipe. This evening, I have smoked more
than ordinary. And I shall, accord ingly, behold unwonted
phantoms, phantoms which are to recent shades what those
shades are to living beings.

I have, just this moment, happened upon the usual circle of
this-century ghosts. They are decent and more or less pitiable
apparitions, in no wise strange or terrible. Their skeletons clatter
lightly in the breeze, while the tatters of their shrouds and funeral
vestments still flutter about them.

But now, they are seeking a frightened earth-refuge in their
tombs, alarmed by the coming of specters from the century
before. For I can discern, emerging from the cypresses, a whole
dolorous band of barely perceptible beings, trailing after them
ropes, scimitars and bow-strings. These are the ones who
have been put to death. I know them well, for they are always
revealed to me with the fiftieth pipe. They are slaves, eunuchs
and faithless wives. Their diaphanous bones no longer make
any noise as they clatter against each other; and I am scarcely
able to distinguish the effaced outlines of their former bodies.

Nevertheless, I can read suffering and fear upon their faces; and I make note of the fact that, in their droll dance, they are careful to avoid the terrace with the fttbig lindens,—careful, also, to avoid the dark lane which leads to the funereal spindle-tree. Through out all eternity, the executioner's victims continue to fear the executioner and to flee his terrible shade. The tomb remains deserted, and the old prince goes on sleeping his deep, untroubled sleep. And yet, as I look more closely, it seems to me that, over there, the branches of that bush are shuddering, and \ can see the skeleton of a dog roaming about.

More, more opium. I wish, today, to go all the way to that frontier which separates drunkenness from death.

* * *

I have smoked a hundred pipes, all of them heap ing ones, and my opium is a powerful mixture of Yunnan and Benares. Those ties which, but recent ly, bound me to my fleshly rags and tatters,— those ties have just snapped; and in that flesh there remains barely the power to lift the bamboo and to cook the drug over the flame.

The well nigh immaterial substance of my soul is free; and I now wander, vagabond-like and at will, over the greensward of the park. I wish to view the tomb of the decapitated Greek prince, and to see why it is, the branches and the leaves of the trees are shud dering so....

* * *

It is, indeed, he. His tall figure brings terror to the trembling cypresses. I behold him rising from his grave, the blood still streaming frorrrrm his severed neck. His vestments, embroidered in fine gold, gleam brilli-antly, despite the putrescence of the dank soil, as his decapitated head gnashes its teeth beside him.

He is walking now. The terror-stricken phantoms have gone back to nothingness.

He drags his head after him, by the hair. I can hear the white hairs of his beard catching on the brambles of the path. Red drops coagulate upon the sand, and the skeleton-dog sneaks up to sniff them.

He has taken the center lane, the one that leads to the Red Palace. But at the door, the odor of the drug stands guard; and he goes on, without pausing. He is now climbing the marble stairs which lead to the terrace,—the terrace with the big lindens, the terrace soaked in blood, in ancient blood.

He mounts with exceedingly slow steps,—with the gait of a prince and of a master. In the light of the stars, his hands may be seen gleaming with rings, and occasionally, he lays one of his hands, imperiously, upon a beam or a baluster.

He mounts. The dog trots after him, at a distance, and sometimes pauses, irresolutely. The wide steps lead from lanes to cornices. In the shadows, at the top of the steep flight, the Red Palace is barely dis tinguishable, and nothing is to be perceived except the sea, beating lugubriously at the bottom.

Up above, the terrace rises like a scaffold. The lindens cover it with a veil of black leaves, and leprous mosses creep about its base like a funeral garment.

The headless silhouette has now reached the last of the steps. I now can see it pulling up short, as in front of a precipice, as the skeleton-dog, trembling with fright, turns and flees, with fantastic leaps and bounds, through the thicket. The severed head upon the ground gives a weird start, each of its hairs brist ling with horror.

As I draw near, anxious to discover the cause of all this terror, the phantom wavers and becomes a dis-colored apparition. I already can see through it; it it no more than a grayish vapor, with a few scraps of gilt still gleaming here and there, and with some lit tle tinseling of embroidery and jewels. Then, all be comes attenuated and effaced, blending with the darkness of night. The severed head remains behind for a few seconds, the gleam of its white eyes surviv ing the loss of bodily contours. Then, all disappears, and nothing is left but the night.

The terrace is absolutely dark. The terrified will-o'-the-Wisps have retired underground. The dead trunks of the lindens shiver with fright, and little fragments of bark slip from them, to take hiding under the moss.

And yet, the saddened phantoms wandering there are by no means terrifying. I can see them: the bodies of two slaughtered infants, silently weeping. And nothing more. . . .

Yes, there are other shadows still, confused, inter-mingled, dark, very near to nothingness. That one there is dragging itself along on the ground; that one is groveling in the red slime;—it is, in short, a horrible pulp of amputated members, bloodless heads, and hearts snatched from their bosoms. Unspeakable crimes emerge pell-mell from the fattened earth. And now, I know, I know.... I have gone down the whole course of the centuries. And here comes, from out the ancient mist, a creature spilling all its blood.

Here it is. . . . It is like a giant bat, a female bat, grazing the trees in its shaggy flight. I can make out the mortal beauty of its love-inspiring face, and the opulence of that sombre hair, strewn with venomous serpents.

I recognize her. Her name is Medea. It is here that she gathers her philters, here that she poisons and rends. It is here that the blond hero, the golden-haired conqueror, throws her palpitating upon the amorous grass.—It is here that she takes vengeance upon the flesh of her flesh, and pays each stolen kiss with an infant's corpse.

* * *

Can it be that my body, down there in the fumerie of the Red Palace, is now wholly dead?

Euximograde, October 24, 1902.

SIXTH PERIOD

The Nightmare

IT IS the end, the end of everything. . . .

It has been eight, nine, how many? forty days? that I have had nothing to eat,—or drink: my throat no longer knows the taste of tea; there is something on the threshold that stops it, something like dross, like opium, something—I do not know what. It has been forty days, or forty months, that I have had no tea to drink,—and nothing else whatsoever, naturally, —and how many years since I last slept?

I do not know. I know nothing any more. Nothing any more.

Good heavens! in order to know, to reckon, to attain some sort of certitude concerning anything, it would be necessary,—would it not?—to see, to hear, to feel,—to make use, in short, of what men call their senses, their five senses? Five? Are there five? It makes little difference, after all.—Yes, it would be necessary to do all that. But I have no more senses. It has been a long time, indeed, since I had any. I cannot see. I have looked too long at the lamp, and at the yellow opium, budding and crackling above the lamp.—I have looked too long into the night, opening wide my horrified eyes in an effort to compel them to see what men do not see,—the beyond, the pale and terrifying world of phantoms;—my eyes have seen them, and that is why, now, they no longer see anything,—except the lamp, the opium-lamp.—Yes, the phantoms. ... As a matter of fact, that is not true; there are no phantoms since I have ceased to see them. An hallucination, an hallucination which has disappeared, that is all.

I am well enough aware that there are no phantoms. Alas! There
is nothing. There is Nothingness. . . .

I can no longer hear, either. I have listened too intently to the
sounds out of the silence, sounds which no one ever heard except
myself, who am about to die;—sounds made by the motionless
air, and by. the earth in repose, and by the infinite little beings
who live and die upon the earth. And the buzzing that comes
from it all has embedded itself so formidably into my ears that
I no longer have any ear-drums left. And now, no sound from
without reaches my solitude. My solitary brain clamors and
howls in the middle of my cranium,—so loudly that all within
me is shattered, as my bones crumble to dust,—that dust which I
so soon shall be.

Tell me, do you think that dust will smell of opium? No? And
yet, I have smoked much. Three, four, a hundred pipes a day,—or
more, even, who knows?

I no longer see, and I no longer hear. And so it is with
everything. There is not one human sensation left me, not one
human action of which I am capable. Not one, not one. Nothing.
Ah! yes, one thing, a verb: to suffer.

Oh, the suffering that I endure! Oh, the fire which rends and
devastates my entrails, reddening them to a white heat! Inside
me, there is a flaming wound, a wound that begins at my throat
and ends lower down than my ankles; a wound that spares
nothing, neither vein nor bowel, a wound that is perpetually
spouting flames. The rivers, lakes, the sea and all the oceans
might roll over those flames without extinguishing them. And
it is forever, forever, with no pause, no respite, no sleep. All the
way to nothingness, a more terrifying nothingness. . . .

Upon my skin, the opium's itch has bitten in so deeply that
I no longer have any epidermis left: I have torn it all away, with
my fingernails.

And if that were all! If there were nothing more!

There is the hunger and thirst after opium. Days and days passed without eating or drinking,—all that is nothing, less than nothing:—a pleasure. But an hour without opium, that, that is the terrible, the unutterable thing, the one disease for which there is no cure. It cannot be cured, for the reason that satiety itself does not extinguish such a thirst. Before smoking, I am dying from need of opium, and I die again afterwards, and while I am smoking, and always. My body is in agony from the moment I abandon the pipe. I am that damned one who, in seeking comfort from burning coals, finds only molten lead.

The damned one. That is it; that is exactly it. The Gehenna in which I abide has two penalties, adds insult to injury: to disease of body disease of soul; to the fire, the nightmare.

At first,—how long a time ago it was!—I had only brief sleeping spells, prostrations lasting a few hours, a few minutes, between two intoxications;—a deadening slumber, utterly prostrating, from which I arose more fatigued than by the most violent of love-embraces;—but real sleep, none the less, free of phantasmagoric images, closed to the terrors of the world without. Then, day would come, with its feverish lethargies and its deliriums, filled with bewilderments, atrocities and apocalypses. And it was then that a sort of dismaying proportion was set up: to the degree in which opium abbreviated, cut short my moments of repose,—for it was still repose, almost,—in a corresponding degree, that same opium began filling, heaping and cramming those moments with more bewilderments, with more atrocities and with more apocalypses. Until the superhuman limit of this series, which no mathematician ever will be able to add up, was reached at last: that limit where sleep is reduced to zero and nightmare is raised to a corre sponding and inverse power,—one divided by zero equals: infinity: $1/0 = 00$.

I do not sleep any more. And nightmare, overstepping the too restricted confines of my slumber, now has spread over all my day. I dream all the time, and that is vastly more atrocious.

Nightmare. No one except opium-smokers ever will know what a nightmare is.

I have heard people say: Last night, I had a frightful dream: the walls came together and crushed me. Or, it may be: I fell down a precipice. Or, perhaps: I saw my wife and children being tortured, without being able to rescue them. And those persons will raise their hands to their eyes and remark with horror: What a nightmare!

In my own nightmare, there is neither precipice, nor wall, nor wife, nor children. There is the void, nothingness and the night. There is the awful reality of death,—so near, so near, that the condemned man waiting for the guillotine never glimpses eternity so close up as I.

Death, round about me, roves and stagnates. It blocks door and window; it crawls across the mat; it flowers into atmospheric molecules; it enters my lungs, along with the black smoke; and when I emit the smoke, it does not come forth.

Here is a chap who is already dead, like myself. They have tossed him into a well. But wait, where is that well, in reality?

That makes no difference. They have tossed him into a well. There is an eel at the bottom of the well'.

* * *

An eel or a watersnake?—Or a water-snake!—Do you hear?

The snake has bitten the corpse.—It, in turn, is dead— naturally. They fished it up because it was an eel. And the cat has bitten the eel. The cat! Do you hear?

It is here, the cat. Big as a tiger,—naturally. But with the bead of a very small kitten. It is dying. It whirls about the lamp. I whirl, too,—in an opposite diwction. Ve are going to meet ... we are going to meet. . . .

Ha! ha! ha! Help. . . .

THE END

CPSIA information can be obtained at www.ICGtesting.com
Printed in the USA
LVOW11s1221080316

478238LV00005B/22/P